Murder
at
Rainbow Falls

Tommy Lovelace
and
Betty Streett

Forward Movement Publications
Cincinnati, Ohio

Illustrations
Mara D. Califf

Cover Art
Barron Krody

Cover Photo
© Chuck Summers:
Contemplative Images

©1999
Forward Movement Publications
412 Sycamore Street
Cincinnati, Ohio 45202
USA

Murder at Rainbow Falls *is dedicated to*
Ruth Vietch Evans, our great-grandmother
and mother, who taught her family
to love nature, to love adventure
and, best of all, to love God.

CONTENTS

CHAPTER ONE

The Mountain

The squeaky old van chugged toward the mountain. It was late spring, already hot and humid in the east Tennessee foothills, and the van's air conditioner had died years ago. Six sweating kids plus the driver were packed inside, those in the middle straining toward the open windows, futilely hoping for a breath of cooler air. Two of the occupants would soon witness a murder.

Tommy Stratton sat up front next to his eighteen-year-old aunt, Corbin, who was both driver and camp counselor. A veteran camper, Corbin had survived several seasons in the Tennessee mountains attending the Pioneer Camp sponsored by her church. This was Tommy's first time camping, and he wasn't exactly enthusiastic. Ever since he became captain of his seventh grade football team, he saw himself as tough and cool, and thought going to camp was geeky. He had tried to get out of it, but his mom had made him go!

Leaning against the door, his head stuck as far out the window as he thought Corbin would allow, Tommy sneaked occasional glances at his aunt. She was five years older and had been more like his sister when they were younger. Now there was a mystery about her. He felt he didn't know her well anymore. Physically, they were very unlike. She had long blond hair; his was almost black. Her eyes were grey, his were blue like his mom's and grandmother's. She was tall and slender; he was short and slightly pudgy. Adults told him he hadn't had his growth spurt yet, and that when he did he'd shoot up like a bean stalk and lose his baby fat. He didn't quite believe them, although he wanted to.

Corbin seemed to be reading his mind. "Tommy, this is a great place for a summer camp. You'll love it," she shouted over the roar of the engine.

"Yeah, sure, whatever," Tommy replied, almost under his breath. "Rainbow Falls," he muttered to himself. "What a geeky name. I can see the headline in the school paper: The captain of the football team goes to Rainbow Falls Summer Camp. Nuts, *Rambo* Falls should be where I'm going!"

Rip Ferris was half in the seat behind Tommy, head hanging out the window, short brown hair flattened by the wind. He pulled himself inside long enough to scream at Tommy, "This is great! You and me and Bill are going camping in the mountains. Look at that mountain, Tommy. We'll be up on the top in just a few minutes." Rip and his brother Bill were Corbin's neighbors, and the three boys were constant companions for several weeks every summer when Tommy visited Corbin and his grandparents. This was the first time they had all been to camp together, but Rip and Bill had been rafting in the east Tennessee mountains with their dad, so they were really excited.

"Oh, joy," was Tommy's cynical response.

Bill's slightly squeaky, slightly hoarse voice piped in, "And we're going to be in the same counseling group with Corbin!" Corbin had been a soccer star at the local high school, and was one of Bill's heroes. Being the younger of the two brothers, Bill had lost the fight for the window seat. His blond hair was dark with sweat.

Rip hadn't picked up on Tommy's less than positive attitude. "We're going white water rafting on the Ocoee. My dad says the Summer Olympic teams hold competition on the Ocoee. Dad hasn't taken us on the Ocoee yet; Bill wasn't big enough. Did y'all know someone died on the Ocoee last year?"

This information, engaged Tommy's attention. It was one thing to butt heads on a football field, another to risk your life in a rubber raft on white water. "Is that true?" he asked Corbin. "Did someone really die on the Ocoee?"

Corbin resisted throwing Rip a disapproving frown. "It's true, Tommy." Corbin shouted in his direction in order to be heard over the groan of the engine and wind from the windows. "Sometimes people go on the river not knowing what they're doing, or they take unnecessary chances. If we're careful and follow all the rules, we'll be okay." She shot a glance at Tommy, detecting his ill humor, knowing that underneath his cynicism there was a bright, sensitive young man who was afraid of heights, an inheritance from his mom and grandmother. Now she detected a possible growing fear of white water rafting. If that was so she wanted to help him gain some confidence. "Just wait till you see the cliff we're going to climb and rappel from," she said. "Can you believe it, the first time I came to camp here, I, the great Corbin England, was afraid to rappel. The second year I said my prayers, got my courage up and did it. But I climbed the rock the first year. You may be braver than I, and repel the first time out! The gear is easy to use, and it's completely safe."

She turned the van off the main highway and onto the narrow mountain road which would take them to the top. The van slowed as it began its climb up the mountainside. Corbin lowered the gear and got a little more power. Her dad had the engine overhauled and the brakes relined before they left home, but the van didn't seem to have the power it should.

"I don't see where climbing a mountain hanging on a harness with ropes is any challenge," was Tommy's carefully considered response. "If you're completely safe, what fun is it? I'd just as soon head out on my own, and climb the mountain without all that junk tied around me."

"No!" Bill squeaked. "That's too dangerous. You

can't go out alone. There's bears on the mountain."

"I doubt there are any bears," Tommy said. "The place is probably crawling with people. Corbin says there's even a college there."

Corbin smiled at the picture of Pioneer Camp Tommy must have in his mind. "It's a university; that's even bigger than a college," she said. "My dad, your Big Daddy, went to school there. But where we're going, there are still bears, and we have to look out for them."

The prehistoric van was climbing so slowly the kids couldn't help noticing the beauty of the mountain. Leaves on the trees and shrubs wore the light, bright greens of spring, and the branches danced together as the wind stirred them. Wild flowers of all colors and sizes sprang up along the edge of the road. Redbud and dogwood trees bloomed in the shade of the forest. Bugs buzzed among the cool shadows of the trees, then darted out into the bright sunshine, often narrowly missing the windshield of the creeping vehicle.

"Corbin, I want my tent close to the showers," Vanessa called out from the middle of the back of the van where she sat alone. She was one of three girls assigned to Corbin's group, and the only one concerned with her appearance. Debbie and Jo'Dee, the other girls, sat together, following the van's progress on a map. Turning together toward Vanessa, they gave her a disgusted look. Both girls enjoyed dressing in jeans, and neither wore makeup. Debbie's red hair was long and straight like Corbin's, and matching red freckles dotted her face and bare arms. Jo'Dee wore her hair naturally also, but cut short in the Afro style, black curls tight against her milk chocolate face.

"Vanessa," Corbin shouted, craning her head as far back as she could while keeping an eye on the road, which was now winding steeply toward the mountain's crest. "You know we won't be the only group there. I expect it'll be first come, first serve as to who gets their tent closest to the facilities."

"Will we be the first ones there?" Vanessa asked.

"We'll be doing good to get there at all," Corbin whispered to herself. She didn't want the kids to panic, but the temperature dial on the van's console was moving into the red. She wondered if she was seeing steam or only heat waves above the hood. Could it be they hadn't checked the hoses? More loudly she responded to Vanessa, "I doubt it. We got a late start because we had to wait on some of you." She caught the younger girl's concerned face in the van's rear-view mirror. "And it was you, Vanessa, we had to wait for the longest!"

Corbin wondered about the progress of the other campers. She'd driven her dad's old van, picking up Vanessa, Jo'Dee and Debbie, who lived in the neighborhood. Two more van loads started from the church, but she had no idea where they might be. And she needed to know. Now there was no doubt! The engine was smoking. Corbin down shifted and braked, pulling over to the side of the road. It didn't take much to stop the old vehicle. She pulled the emergency brake, as the kids crowded to the front.

"What's wrong, why are we stopping?" everyone asked at once.

"Get back and give me some breathing room and I'll tell you," Corbin said, gently pushing them away. "The van's running hot. I've got to look under the hood and see if I can tell what's causing it and if I can do anything about it."

"Let me help," Rip said, leaning over Corbin's shoulder. "I help my dad with motors all the time."

"We'll all get out," Corbin said. "Everyone stay off the road. Don't go anywhere! And Rip, don't touch the hood of the van. It's hot!"

All the kids spilled out. None of them stayed off the road. Everyone wanted to see the engine and offer less than helpful advice.

"I won't open the hood until you're all off the road, together and quiet!" Corbin shouted over the din of excited voices. She leaned against the door of the van, folding her arms across her chest. Seeing she meant business, the kids dispersed quietly to the roadside.

Corbin felt inside the grill to find the latch. She took her kerchief from her head where she had tied it to keep sweat from running into her eyes, wrapped it around her hand and opened the dented hood. Steam bellowed up, and when it cleared, she could see that the radiator hose was ruptured. A large, jagged tear ran down its side. "This van isn't going another foot!" Corbin thought to herself, wondering how to handle the emergency. She didn't want to make all the kids walk the rest of the way up the mountain in the afternoon heat, without water in their canteens and griping with every step, but she hated to leave them alone. "Lord," she silently prayed, "I don't have any other choices unless you supply us with one, and it looks like the safest thing to do is to take them along. Please keep us safe, and don't let them complain too much."

Before she finished the prayer, they heard the sound of another engine. The vehicle was still out of sight, but was clearly winding in their direction. As it came around the curve of the mountain, Corbin got a look at the driver; it was Jon, the senior counselor. She had been praying for a miracle, and here it was. "It's Jon," she cried. "Get your things out of the van. We're saved!" The girls cheered, the boys high fived, and everyone ran to get their belongings as the van approached. It would be crowded, but they could finish their journey together on wheels.

As the rescue vehicle slowed to a stop, the kids rushed the door, all trying to get in at once. Corbin was reminded of unruly crowds at British soccer games, and shouted for them to stop. One at a time they climbed in, dragging their gear behind them, Corbin bringing up the rear. "The radiator hose is done for," she told Jon as she pulled herself up the high step.

Luckily for Corbin's crew, the kids in Jon's van had been even later than Vanessa. As the leader and the only older man in the group, Jon had been embarrassed at being so late until he spied the disabled van around the curve of the road. Now he felt better. Smiling at Corbin he said, "You did well to keep your gaggle of geese together. We'll be able to get someone from Ocoee to come up and fix the hose. I'll call AAA and they'll locate the closest tow truck for us." He reached in a bag for his car phone.

"What a relief to have a phone," said Corbin. "My dad told me to get one, but I didn't believe I'd need it. Tell them I left the key in the ignition. There's no chance anyone is going to drive it off." Corbin smiled back at Jon. She really liked him. He was a big man, over six feet tall, but with warm, brown puppy eyes and a sweet smile. "It's a university town. There's got to be an auto mechanic there with all the kids with broken down cars. Good grief! Your air conditioner actually works."

The sardine-packed van lumbered up the rest of the steep grade, then purred along the short, dirt road to the camp area. Kids fell out like circus clowns spilling from a Volkswagen bug. David, the third counselor, was impatiently waiting with his group; they all ran up to the van and crowded around. Like Corbin, David was eighteen, smart, blond, and loved the mountains. Just a little taller than Corbin, he had serious hazel eyes. "Where have you been?" they all asked. "What took you so long?"

"Everything's okay," Jon said and changed the subject; he was a man of few words and didn't want to go into long explanations. "It's late, and we need firewood. We've got to collect it before dark. Counselors, take someone from your group and spread out. Get the driest wood you can find and get it back quick! The rest of us will pitch the tents."

David and Corbin looked around for helpers. "Let's go," David said, pointing to Calvin, a black-headed, doe-eyed boy in his group and motioning for him to follow. Tommy was standing next to Corbin, so she put her hand on his shoulder. "Come on," she said. "I know where to go. This way!"

She and Tommy moved quickly out of the campsite and into the brush, while David and Calvin crossed the road and headed in the opposite direction. Corbin easily located the trail she knew so well. It led to the beautiful waterfall that gave the camp its name. Tommy followed close behind on the narrow trail. Their eyes searched the forest floor for dry wood as they walked.

"There's some," Tommy called out, darting off the path to get it.

"No, Tommy," Corbin directed. "Wait until we come back, just remember where you saw it. We'll pick up what we find at the end of the path, then collect the rest as we walk back. That way we don't have to carry everything both ways."

The two continued silently, Tommy's eyes searching the underbrush for dead wood. Suddenly, he crashed into Corbin's back. She had stopped silently, gazing at something straight ahead. "Look out," she said.

"What are you doing?" Tommy asked.

"I'm looking at something wonderful."

Tommy came around her, looking where she was pointing. It *was* wonderful. Just ahead of them the woods ended. Bare rock formed a horseshoe where water from a stream spilled over, falling 200 feet to a dark pool. A huge rainbow hung in the damp spray above the half-circle. Its sparkling colors danced in the sunlight, moving through the spectrum from red to violet.

"Gee," was all Tommy could say.

"What?" Corbin said. "Can this be? Are you speechless?"

"This is awesome," Tommy said.

"It *is* beautiful. This is one reason I wanted you to come. I wanted you to see this," Corbin told him with a hug. Knowing Tommy wouldn't be able to tolerate too much sentimentality, she challenged him to follow her down a trail leading to the bottom of the falls. Trees and brush lined both sides of the slippery trail, so Tommy didn't sense the height and felt little fear as he half-slid down behind her. Moving almost silently, they heard the roar of water falling to its cool, dark destination.

At the bottom they walked to the edge of the churning, black pool. As they stood on the wet rocks and stared into its depths, the falling water almost hypnotized them. Light from above was dimming; the rainbow was fading. Bright leaves sailing on the surface of the water turned darker and darker. Corbin strained her eyes toward the top of the falls to get a last look at the rainbow. "Look up, Tommy. The light's going; the rainbow will disappear soon."

Tommy followed her gaze, still enchanted with his surroundings. As they watched the fading colors, they saw the outline of a figure moving from the shadow of a tree onto the horseshoe rock high above them. At first Corbin thought it was a fellow counselor, but the silhouette wasn't quite the right shape. It looked strange. Suddenly the figure seemed to separate in two, and one of the pieces fell heavily, bouncing off the rocks, flying toward them.

It landed on the rocks in front of them, part of it splashing into the black water. It was a body. Amazed and terrified, Corbin and Tommy quickly looked again to the top of the ledge. The figure was still there, seeming to peer down into the gorge. They could see only the outline of a man against the pale glow of twilight. How clearly, they wondered, could he see them?

Chapter Two

The Murder

Corbin was sure the man who fell into the pool was unconscious, if not dead. And she was sure he was unconscious before he went over the falls. Otherwise he would have screamed or called out. He had fallen limply, bouncing off the rocks like a rag doll. She pulled Tommy back with her into the forest's darker shadows, fearful of the man standing silently above.

"What are you doing?" Tommy shouted, jerking his arm free of her hand, his face scrunched up in indignation. At age twelve, there was nothing he hated worse than being shoved around by anyone larger or older than himself.

"I'm not sure," Corbin replied in a whisper, although no one could have heard her over the roar of the waters. "I don't think that man fell off the cliff on his own." Forming her thoughts as she talked she continued, "I think the man at the top threw him over. Please just be still and quiet a minute. Lets see what he does."

Tommy still felt hurt by being unwillingly dragged back among the trees by his aunt, but he did as he was told. They both looked up to the top of the rock. The figure was gone. The ledge was empty.

"What do we do?" Tommy whispered. Reality was setting in. Now he was glad to have someone even slightly older making decisions.

"I've got to get to the man to see if he's alive—see if we can help." Corbin said. She had the knack of staying cool in a crisis, then collapsing after everything was over. "Stay here. If you see anyone come back to the ledge or coming down the rocks, call me."

"If you think I'm staying here by myself, you're crazy," Tommy almost screamed. "Anyway, you can't pull that big man out by yourself." He started for the falls.

"Wait," Corbin said. "And be quiet!" She strained her eyes and ears, looking and listening toward the ledge, then down the steep rock trail. With the dimming light, a chorus of night birds, tree and bull frogs had joined a symphony of crickets, cicadas and katydids. A lone hoot owl woke and added his woeful voice, sending a shiver down Corbin's back. "Okay, lets go," she said.

They crept stealthily back to the pool. The body bobbed against the rocks. The man lay face down, half in, half out of the pool. His long black hair floated about his head, which wagged unnaturally in the waves. His wet jacket and jeans clung to his body. He was a big man. Corbin had been taught lifesaving and first aid but now she was unable to move, frozen to the spot. She was afraid the man was dead, and she had never touched a dead person.

"Should we go up and get some help?" Tommy asked reasonably, curiosity overcoming dread as he stepped to the edge of the water, leaning over to look at the floating form.

His question revived Corbin's courage and she went into action. "We've got to get him out of the water," she said. "Help me pull him up onto the rocks."

She reached into the cold water and grabbed an arm, while Tommy pulled on the man's jacket. Getting him out of the pool was a struggle, especially with the added weight of the wet clothes. Both Corbin and Tommy were physically fit, but even so it required all their strength to bring him even partially up onto the rocks.

The man's back was toward Corbin, his face still hidden by his hair. An arm and part of a shoulder were still in the water. She gingerly touched his neck hoping to find a pulse, but knowing by the way the head lay on its side that something was badly wrong. The flesh was cold and damp, there was no warmth, no pulse, no life.

"He's dead," she said.

"Are you sure?"

"Dead sure," she said, unconscious of the pun.

"Good grief," Tommy responded. "We've got to get out of here and tell someone."

"Do we leave his body here alone?" she asked, mostly to herself.

"I'm not staying here, and I can't find the camp by myself," Tommy almost cried, tears welling up in his deep blue eyes. Now he was angry at the man and at Corbin. His stress tolerance was stretched to the limit.

"You're right," she said. "We'll both go back to the camp. We've got to leave him here. We've got to hurry. I don't have a flashlight, and it'll be dark as sin before we get to the top. We need to say a prayer for him first." Corbin bowed her head and Tommy self-consciously followed suit. He seldom prayed on his own unless the score was close in a football game. "Lord," she prayed, "we don't know this man and I'm not a minister, but please have mercy on him, and take him into your heavenly kingdom. And, please don't let any wild animals get to his body before we get back with help. Amen."

Corbin turned and moved quickly toward the slippery rock path they had come down earlier. Tommy followed closely, not daring to look back at the black, solitary shape they had left at the pool side. Climbing fast, they repeatedly slipped and lost their footing. Mud smeared their arms, legs, faces and clothing. Scrapes on Tommy's knees filled with it; Corbin's hair turned dark with it. They grabbed bushes and vines to pull themselves along. It wouldn't occur to Corbin until the next day that some of what they grabbed might have been poison ivy. In a matter of minutes they were over the top, running through the forest toward the campsite.

The light of the huge campfire danced in the dark as they came out of the tall trees and into the clearing. Unbelievably, everyone was sitting around it, cooking, eating, talking and laughing. Wieners were being roasted. Cokes, Pepsis and Sprites were being passed around and opened. In the bright firelight, Tommy saw Rip with one end of a huge hot dog in his mouth, the other end dripping ketchup onto his shirt. Bill was teasing Vanessa with a flaming marshmallow at the end of a coat hanger. "They don't know," Tommy thought to himself. "They think everything's all right!"

"Someone's dead," Corbin screamed out as she ran.

Tommy ran past her, shouting, "There's a dead man in the pool down under the falls."

CHAPTER THREE

The Sheriff

Campers and counselors turned their heads to look at the raving maniacs. They all assumed it was a joke.

"Where on earth did you two go?" Jon asked, somewhat angrily. "David and Calvin got back ages ago. Looking at their empty arms he added, "You didn't even bring any wood." Corbin's irresponsibility surprised him.

"Yeah, where's your wood?" a general cry went up, along with "Where have you been?"

"It's true!" Corbin gasped. "There's a dead man in the pool at the falls. Someone threw him in. We saw it. We've got to get the police." She was almost crying with frustration. It never occurred to her they wouldn't believe them.

Seeing tears forming in Corbin's eyes, Jon began to

take them seriously. "How do you know the person's dead?" he asked.

"Tommy and I pulled him out of the water and I felt his neck for a pulse. He's dead. You've got to get the police down there, now!"

"He's dead. He's *really* dead!" Tommy affirmed breathlessly.

Fire and dinner forgotten, the rest of the campers crowded around. Rip and Bill pushed their way to Tommy's side. He was their best friend, and they weren't going to miss anything.

"What happened?" Rip asked.

"Did you *see* someone kill him?" Bill wanted to know, blue eyes wide with awe.

"We saw someone throw him off the cliff," Tommy said.

"Who did it? Who threw him over?" Vanessa asked.

"We don't know who it was," Tommy answered, so excited he was willing to respond to a girl. "It was too dark to get a good look at him, but he was big."

"We've got to get the police," Corbin said, beginning to feel like a broken record. "Where's the car phone?"

"It's in the van," Jon said. "Up here, we don't call the police. We call the sheriff. Do you think this part of Tennessee has 911?"

"Try it," Corbin suggested.

Everyone agreed this was a good idea. They fell silent as Jon opened his van, pulled out the phone and punched in the numbers.

"It's ringing," he said.

"Thank goodness," Corbin said. She would feel such relief when the "authorities" showed up. Somehow she felt responsible for everything until then.

"This is Jon Anderson. I'm on a car phone at Gizzard Trail camp grounds, on the Ocoee Domain. One of our counselors has a dead body to report in the pool at the bottom of Rainbow Falls. We need the sheriff immediately."

Everything was quiet while the 911 operator tried to decide if the call was real or a hoax. "The sheriff is a busy man," she said. "I don't want to call him way out there for nothing."

Jon straightened up and used his deep voice. "I assure you, we're a bona fide church-sponsored camping group. We come up here every year. We need the sheriff and we need him *now.*"

Jon's voice persuaded her. After asking for his van tag number and the car phone number, she agreed to get the sheriff immediately.

"They're on the way," he said.

"What do we do in the meantime?" Corbin asked. She could visualize the body by the pool, with wild animals everywhere.

"I don't know," Jon admitted, rubbing his huge hand through his hair, a trait of his whenever he was nervous or confused. "I've never had anything like this happen before."

"How long will it take the sheriff to get here?" Tommy asked, not yet realizing that grown men don't like to be asked too many questions they can't answer.

"I don't know that, either," Jon said, irritation in his voice. "In all the years I've come here, I've never had to call him. I have no idea how long it'll take him to get way up here. I don't even know where he's coming from!"

"Sorry," Tommy said, slightly hurt by Jon's tone.

"Let's call her back and ask," Corbin sensibly offered, forgetting that grown men dislike asking for information almost as much as they dislike admitting they don't have it.

Jon's pride was saved by the ringing car phone. After a brief conversation, he was relieved to report that the sheriff had been located nearby and would be there shortly.

"Okay," he said. "We need to decide what to do when he gets here. Corbin, I'm afraid you'll have to go down with him. You'll need to show him the way and report exactly what you saw."

"I've got to go back, too," Tommy insisted. "I saw everything, too. I may have seen something she didn't!" As he was taking a breath to continue, Jon interrupted him.

"Not a chance." he said. "I want everyone to stay together. I'm not even going. I'm going to stay here with you guys." Jon chose his words carefully, not wanting to frighten the kids by implying there was danger. He had begun to think about the man they saw at the top of the cliff, wondering if he might still be in the area.

Bill blurted out the question Jon had decided not to ask, "Did he see you? Did the killer see you?"

Corbin and Tommy looked at each other. Once more, the awfulness of the events overcame them as they recalled the dark, lone figure at the top of the falls. Together they turned to Bill and said sadly, "We don't know."

The wail of a siren brought them back to the present. Everyone ran to the road and strained to see the sheriff's vehicle coming toward the clearing. Except for the flashing blue lights, the car was nearly invisible.

Two men jumped out almost before the car stopped—the driver, small, wearing a huge Stetson hat, the other bareheaded, tall and thin. The driver wore the sheriff's badge. Although shorter, he moved faster than the tall man as they rushed to meet the campers.

"I'm Sheriff Crockett; this here's my deputy," he said, motioning vaguely in the direction of the tall man. "Where's the body?"

Everyone tried to answer at once. Jon held up his hands for quiet. "I'm Jon Anderson; this is my camping group. Corbin, one of our counselors, saw everything and can take you there."

"Where is he?" the sheriff asked.

"I'm him," Corbin said, stepping up beside Jon.

The sheriff was surprised to see a girl. This was a wilderness campsite. Although he was a Tennessee country boy, he knew just enough about political correctness to try to keep his surprise to himself. "Where's the body," he repeated. Like Jon, apparently the sheriff was another man of few words.

"I'll take you to it," Corbin answered. "Let's go."

Unasked, Jon offered, "I'll stay here with David and the other campers. I had already planned to help keep everything safe up here."

The sheriff gave him a nod. "After you," he said to Corbin, removing a huge flashlight from a hook on his belt and turning it on.

Sensing the sheriff's attitude toward women, Corbin decided to give him a run for his money, and began to stride quickly through the brush. The deputy, with his own light, followed them, hurrying to keep up.

The night was dark. Black clouds covered the moon and stars. They reached the falls in what seemed to be no time. Corbin went first, stepping and occasionally fanny scooting down the steep descent. The less agile men had to turn and face the wet rocks, feeling their way down, clinging to branches and vines, the light from the flashlights waved crazily and uselessly among the trees above them. They fussed in language unfit for polite company.

At the bottom, the men were wet, dirty and unhappy. "Which way?" the sheriff asked grumpily.

"Over there, in the pool," Corbin said. She held her breath, afraid the body would be gone. If it had been dragged off by a large animal, she feared the sheriff wouldn't believe their story.

The flashlights illuminated the surface of the black water as they approached. There it was, on the rocks, partially in the pool, just as she and Tommy had left it. Corbin thanked God under her breath. They walked silently up to the body. The noisy night bird, frog and insect concert continued eerily. The sheriff knelt close by the man's head and, repeating Corbin's earlier action, touched the neck to feel for a pulse. Shaking his head, he looked up at his deputy, then pulled a small phone out of the pocket of his big jacket. The top flipped up, resembling an old *Star Trek* communication device.

"This is sheriff Crockett," he yelled into the little phone; Corbin wondered if he felt he had to shout all the way back to his office, if that was where he was calling. "I've got a dead body at the bottom of Rainbow Falls. I'm going to need the forensic team. Tell 'em to just stay at the campsite 'til I get there. They'll see the fire from the road. And the hospital's going to have to fly in their helicopter to pick up the body. I don't see any other way to git it out of this holler. They'll need extra line."

He listened restlessly as someone seemed to argue with him on the other end. "I don't care who's on leave, git aholt of 'em and git 'em here," he said. "And I don't want to be waitin' in this black hole for the chopper forever, neither. Tell 'em to move it, and I mean quick." He snapped the phone together smartly and replaced it in his pocket.

The sheriff looked very tired. He stood up as tall as he could and turned to Corbin. "You say somebody threw this man off the top of the cliff?"

"Yes, sir," Corbin replied. "Should you look in the man's pockets? Maybe he's got some identification."

"I don't need to," the sheriff said wearily. "I know who he is." Turning to the deputy, he said, "Willy, you recognize him?"

"Yes, *sir*! He's the dope dealer we've been trying to catch from over at the university."

Corbin heard the deputy speak for the first time, and for the first time really looked at him. In the bright glow of the flashlight she saw an older man with thinning brown hair and brown skin, deeply wrinkled. But his blue eyes sparkled. Corbin couldn't help but smile at his mud-covered uniform.

"Looks like somebody caught him for us." the sheriff said.

"You mean you've been looking for this guy?" Corbin asked in amazement.

"We weren't looking for him; we knew where he was," the deputy said, smiling. "We were looking to catch him selling cocaine to the college kids." He pulled his camera out from under his jacket and began taking pictures.

"He's been known to us for some time," the sheriff added. "But he was slick. We couldn't get a pigeon to set him up, an' he spotted our state undercover agents. Willy, be sure you get this angle over here. Forensics can't do any good down here, so I want good shots of the body."

"What did the man look like who threw him over?" the deputy asked, stepping into the pool to get a shot of the man's head from above.

"I don't really know. It was dusk. Tommy and I couldn't really see his face, just his outline."

"He was standin' right above you?" the sheriff continued the questioning.

"Yes. We ducked into the trees to keep him from seeing us," Corbin responded. "When we looked back, he was gone."

"Could you tell how tall he was, or what he had on?" the sheriff asked.

"He seemed about as tall as the man he threw in, I think, and he looked like he had on jeans and a dark jacket."

The deputy was staring down at the body. "This doesn't look like a drug war killing," he said, shaking his head.

"How can you tell?" Corbin asked. Although she knew it wasn't exactly nice, she was losing sympathy for the dead man.

"In a drug war, little girl, the killers don't hide the body," the sheriff said.

"They show off the bodies, so everybody'll know how bad they are and be scared of them." the deputy explained.

"Were you and your friend in deep shadows when you saw the man at the top?" the sheriff asked.

"No, not at first. That's why I pulled Tommy back into the trees."

"Then he could've seen you." The Sheriff looked even more unhappy.

A loud whacking noise drowned out the sound of the serenading night animals. Suddenly, flashing lights came over them. The sheriff looked up, shading his eyes with his hand. "It's the hospital chopper," he said. "For once they're on time."

CHAPTER FOUR

Forensics and a Helicopter

Back at the campsite, Jon and David had their hands full trying to calm down the kids. They had long ago given up any hope of getting them to finish their supper. They were far too excited to be interested in food, even campfire hot dogs! Tommy had become a celebrity. Everyone tried to talk to him at once, asking questions, wanting him to tell the story again and again. Suddenly he was everyone's best friend. Rip and Bill were enjoying a new status as well, since they really were his close friends. They began repeating parts of the story also, almost feeling as if they, too, had been present when the body was thrown over the falls. Only the sound of cars grinding up the mountain and coming toward the campsite diverted the campers' attention.

Headlights cut through the darkness, two cars moved toward the camp and rolled to a stop behind the sheriff's. Men emerged from each one, wearing jeans and jackets, and carrying various cases, lights and photographic equipment. A tall, older man with wisps of white hair led the group, approaching Jon with a sure stride.

"I'm Jack Lovelace. We're the forensic team," he said, holding out his hand to shake.

"I'm really glad you're here," Jon said, eagerly enveloping the man's long, thin hand in his own huge one. Having other adults on the scene was a great relief. David was dependable and a competent veteran of Pioneer Camp, but he was young and almost as excited as the kids. Jon turned toward his younger partner who had joined the little group and said, "This is David, one of our counselors."

The man shook David's hand briskly, making the younger man feel part of the action, and continued, "This is Andy and Frank, and this is Newt." Each man gave a little bow as his name was called. Firelight and shadows danced on their faces, setting their features in eerie motion.

"The sheriff went down to the bottom of the falls with his deputy and Corbin, our other counselor, who saw the body thrown down," David said.

"I saw it fall, too," Tommy contributed, moving into the circle of men.

Jack Lovelace pulled out a phone like the sheriff's

and flipped it open. He punched in numbers, apparently ones he often used, and waited briefly for an answer. "Sheriff," he said. "We're at the campsite. What next?"

He listened silently while the Sheriff gave instructions, then snapped the phone shut. "We're supposed to go over to the edge of the falls, on the south side, to look for tire tracks, foot prints, whatever . . ." His voice was becoming drowned out by an approaching, gradually growing sound.

The helicopter blade whacked loudly through the night sky, lights blazing and bouncing crazily as the chopper neared. Jon was reminded of the scene in *Close Encounters of the Third Kind,* and understood how a chopper at night could be mistaken for a UFO. It disappeared behind the trees, obviously searching for the dark chasm below the falls.

The kids turned and moved as one body, following the helicopter toward the woods. Jon shouted to them to wait; they turned and looked at him and the small group of men, eyes pleading to be allowed to go.

Jon looked at Mr. Lovelace. "What do we do?" he asked, realizing he, too, wanted to see the helicopter at work, perhaps the experience was one which shouldn't be missed.

"We'll need help finding the trail. Just lead on, but keep the kids away from the south side of the falls," the older man responded, almost smiling. Age hadn't altered the kid inside him; he sympathized with their need to be at the falls.

"Okay, let's go!" Jon said, and they all took off through the brush, headed for the woods at a trot.

Lights from the chopper illuminated the pool far below at the base of the falls. The noisy machine was lowering itself into the chasm. Jon warned the kids not to get too close to the edge of the cliff as they gathered round and tried to see down the precipice. They could make out Corbin, the sheriff and deputy, faces straining upward, hands shading their eyes from the bright lights above them. They shouted down to Corbin, but their words were carried off in the wind produced by the falls and the whirling blades. They could just make out the body as a black mass, bobbing in the waves. The sheriff motioned wildly to the helicopter pilot, yelling directions although he knew there was no chance of being heard.

Everyone watched breathlessly as the canvas gurney was lowered from the door in the side of the chopper. It sank silently, waving in the wind as the pilot skillfully maneuvered his hanging in mid-air whirly bird.

Reaching high, the deputy caught the swinging bed and guided it toward the body as it continued to drop. The sheriff rushed up to help, stepping to the other side of the gurney. Together they lugged the dripping body out of the pool and slid it onto the canvas. The sheriff's foot slid out from under him on the wet rocks, sending him and the body splashing back into the black water.

"Oh, good golly!" he mumbled under his breath, then shouted accusingly to his deputy, "Willy, *will* you give me a hand?" Together, they managed to struggle the body back into the gurney and tighten the straps around it. "Up you go," the sheriff hollered toward the hanging helicopter, waving his hand skyward.

The kids above and the group below watched motionlessly as the gurney slowly rose, then disappeared inside the chopper. The kids gave a cheer as the helicopter rose, turned and headed over the trees, toward town and the small hospital. There, later that night, the medical examiner and the forensic team would go over the body carefully for any evidence which might lead them to the killer.

Meanwhile, the forensic team set up their lights and went to work at the south side of the falls. Mr. Lovelace called over to the campers, "Who was it who saw the body go over the falls?"

"It was me," Tommy shouted eagerly. "Do you want me to help?"

"We need for you to show us exactly where the man stood." Mr. Lovelace called back.

He didn't have to ask twice. Tommy ran toward the team, in the excitement and darkness not noticing how close to the ravine's edge he was. Jon called after him to slow down, then ran to catch up with him.

"The man stood here," Tommy said, moving right up to the edge of the falls. Jon reached out and grabbed him by the shirt; they were there to rock climb and rappel, but only when they had on the proper equipment!

When the team trained their lights on the spot,

beams spilled down the abyss. Suddenly, Tommy realized how high up he was. Fear almost paralyzed him. He gulped air and moved back, afraid he might faint, hoping no one would notice the terror in his face. The men moved in front of him, looking carefully at every inch of rock where Tommy had stood. Mr. Lovelace was the photographer. Camera flashing repeatedly, he took pictures from every angle, then began to photograph the other team members as they worked.

"There's a butt!" Frank said. Tommy flinched and moved further back as the man reached down between his feet with a rubber-gloved hand and picked up the burnt end of a cigarette. "You were almost stepping on it," he said as he carefully placed it in a plastic evidence bag. Looking up at Tommy he asked, "Was he smoking?"

"He could have had a cigarette in his mouth, I guess," Tommy said. "He had his hands full with the body."

"We'll check it out, anyway," Frank said thoughtfully as he tucked the bag into one of the cases.

"I've got enough track over here to get a model of the tires," Andy called from a few yards away. "Come on, Newt, and give me a hand. He must have pulled the car off the road. There's a clearing here in the trees leading from the road to the campsite to the falls. He just pulled right up to unload the body, considering the man was probably already dead." Andy loved this part of his job. He felt good about finding real evidence and preserving it. This might be the very thing which would lead to the killer's identification and conviction.

Now that the chopper was gone, the evening was quiet. Even the falling water seemed to make less noise, and the critter concert had ceased except for the lone hoot of the owl. It was too late even for the night animals. Tommy heard voices and the sound of people moving up the steep trail. "Corbin, is that you?" he called.

"We're here!" she shouted up the rock wall. Shortly, her head popped over the rocky ledge.

The deputy and sheriff followed close behind. They were exhausted and muddy. The sheriff was freezing from falling into the water, but was too tired to complain or to even discuss with the team what evidence they'd found. He decided he could wait for the forensics report. "Are you guys finished here?" was all he wanted to know.

"Yep," Jack replied, and the others nodded in agreement.

The sheriff made an impatient sweep of his hand in the direction he thought was toward the camp and began to walk away. "Then let's all move out," he said.

Corbin and David took off in the opposite direction and the others followed. The sheriff looked puzzled, then quickly caught up with them; a good sense of direction wasn't his long suit.

Back in the clearing, the forensic team waved their goodbyes as they lugged their equipment to the waiting cars. The rest of the group headed for the campsite. The fire had died down, but there was plenty of dry wood, so the campers had it blazing again in minutes. David, Corbin and Jon retrieved the hot dogs, fixings, drinks and marshmallows from the coolers, and everyone made room for the visitors to sit up close to the flames.

"Sheriff Crockett," Jon asked, "What do you think? Will the kids be safe here tonight? If not, I guess we could arrange somehow to move into a motel in town." Jon had been silently worrying about this moment all evening; half of him hoped the sheriff would tell them to stay put, and the other half hoped they would be advised to go into the city. At any rate, they couldn't leave Ocoee until Corbin's van was fixed. He hoped AAA had already had it picked up and it was safe in the garage of a local mechanic.

The sheriff considered his words. He hated to take on responsibility for a group of campers, especially kid campers, either way. He doubted there was any real danger from the killer. The sheriff expected whoever it was to be far away by now. "I think you'll be fine right here." he said slowly in his country drawl. His language was a strange mix of simple hillbilly and the complicated words he learned while practicing his profession. "I'm gonna leave Willy out here with you tonight, just to be on the safe side. We'll decide in the mornin' what to do, then."

"You don't think there's any danger?" Jon asked cautiously. He didn't want to frighten the kids unnecessarily.

"Did you see any car lights at all tonight besides

those of me and my men?" the sheriff asked, looking intently at Jon through the firelight. "Did you see any sign at all of anyone else coming up the mountain or anywhere in the area?"

"No, we didn't," Jon answered. The kids nodded as he looked around to check for their response.

"Then there's no danger." Sheriff Crockett was warming up, and beginning to enjoy roasting his hot dog at the end of a coat hanger. He hadn't done this in years. The skin of the wiener was just beginning to burn, and the aroma was wonderful. "The guy who was killed was a dope dealer, but he wadn't killed by a professional. If the killer did chance to see the kids, there's no indication he associated 'em with you. They could've been here with anybody, an' long gone on their way. I'm just leavin' Willy here to be over-precautious. Pass the buns and ketchup, son."

Rip and Bill had seated themselves with Vanessa between them, and had spent much of their time passing dripping hot dogs behind the pretty girl, trailing her dangling hair through the red sauce. Although they were giggling, they were following the conversation when the sheriff looked toward Rip to pass along the items. "Who do you think killed him?" Bill asked, voice squeaky, blue eyes wide, face innocent.

"We don't know, yet," Sheriff Crockett answered, receiving the ketchup from Rip. "But my guess is that it's a buyer. Somebody who bought drugs from him an' maybe owed him money. Somebody prob'ly paid him off permanently!"

Corbin's mind had wandered from the present; she was thinking of tomorrow. "So, what now?" she asked. "Can we stay here and do our camp? We're scheduled to go on the Ocoee tomorrow morning. The whole trip's been planned for months. I don't see any need to quit and go home if the Sheriff says there's no danger."

David was just as committed to staying. Wagon Top Cave was planned for the day after tomorrow. It had been a year since he'd been in a wild cave, and that was the sport he loved most. "I'm with Corbin," he said. "If there's no real threat, let's stay and do what we came here to do."

The kids mustered up their last ounce of energy. "Yeah," everyone said. "Let's stay! Let's do it!"

The sheriff looked thoughtfully at Jon. "Actually, it might help us if you stayed," he said quietly. "The kids didn't see the killer's face, but they saw him. They might remember somethin', they might be able to help us in some way to nail it down when we get a suspect. I expect I'll make an arrest pretty soon. It's a small town. Whoever ran'll be missed quick. That'll identify him, and we'll go wherever he ran to and get him. We'll start with the kids at the university. I'd bet my hat it's one of 'em. This is the kind of chicken way some of them rich kids would handle a real problem."

The campers were amazed at this long speech from the normally silent sheriff, and at his resentment of what he considered "rich kids." He probably wasn't aware that most of the campers would soon be "rich" university types.

"And," he continued, "because I'm askin' you to stay 'round to help, I'm gonna assign Willy, here, to stay with you. He can run home in the mornin' to get a change of clothes. He lives just in the holler over there." The sheriff pointed vaguely off in the wrong direction.

Jon looked at Willy, who smiled and nodded as he popped a smoking marshmallow into his mouth. This was the best assignment he could remember. "Okay," Jon said, looking at his watch, the numbers dancing in the firelight. "You've convinced me. It's late, so we'll bed down now and head out for the river about 8 a.m."

"I'm out-a-here," the sheriff said, rising slowly, almost unwillingly. He would much rather have had Willy's job tonight. Instead, tired as he was, he had to meet up with the medical examiner at the hospital.

Watching the sheriff slowly leave the firelight, the kids began to leave the circle as well. "Whoa," Jon said, softly. "Before we get the tents up and turn in, we need to talk to the one who loves us most."

The kids came back to the circle, and on Jon's cue, joined hands. Rip and Bill were too tired even to try to kid with Vanessa any more. "Let's pray," Jon said. "Dear Father, we've had a hard and strange day. Something very bad has happened. We ask you tonight to have mercy on the man who was killed, and to have mercy on the killer. Please bring him to justice soon, and help him repent of this evil he's done. And, please protect us tonight and while we're here. Help us seek your will in everything we do. In Jesus name, Amen."

Chapter Five

White Water I

The morning's first light was dimmed by rain clouds which, combined with getting to bed so late, caused the campers to oversleep. As soon as they woke up, Willy checked in with the sheriff on the cell phone. There wasn't any real news, so he told his boss they would be riding the Ocoee today if he needed him. After a blessing everyone hurriedly ate cereal out of boxes and glugged down cartons of milk, then loaded up the vans while Willy dashed home for his personal things. It was 9:30 by the time they left; it would be 10 before they put their rafts in the water.

There were three boats. Jon would act as guide in one, David in the second, and Corbin in the third. Crews stayed with their counselors. Inexperienced on the water, Willy was to ride with Jon. Of course Tommy,

Rip and Bill would ride with Corbin, along with Debbie, Jo'Dee and Vanessa. Although more interested in her appearance than Corbin thought necessary, Vanessa was strong, and a good athlete. Corbin had refereed Vanessa's soccer games last fall, and knew she could play as well as any boy on her team. Only one thing was bothering Corbin; the skin between her fingers was beginning to itch.

Tommy," she said. "Are your fingers itching?"

"Nope," he answered. "Why?"

"Mine are. I'm afraid I grabbed some poison ivy last night," she said, wanting to rub them but afraid it would cause the red blisters to pop up sooner.

"Oh," he replied. "I'm not allergic to poison ivy. I used to pull it up and rub it on my face in Boy Scout camp. It'd scare the counselors to death!" He laughed happily, remembering the looks on their faces.

"Help me get our raft down to the river," Corbin called out to the rest of her crew. "Vanessa, bring the paddles from the back of the van."

Rip, Bill and Tommy helped Corbin drag the inflated raft toward the river's edge. Corbin's was the first of the three yellow boats ready to go. She counted the orange life jackets and blue helmets lying brightly inside the raft.

"Tommy," she directed. "Come back to the van with me to get our packs and the food. We're ready to vest."

Rip and Bill jumped into the raft and scrambled for life vests which fit. They hated to wear jackets that were too big or too small. Vanessa arrived, paddles precariously balanced under her arms, and saw what was going on. Dropping her load into the raft, she, too, dived in and started a free-for-all, vest-pulling contest.

"I saw that one first," Bill screeched as Vanessa pulled a particularly new-looking vest from the bottom of the pile. He caught one of the straps and began a tug-of-war.

"You didn't," Vanessa said, voice low and controlled, pulling the vest back in her direction. "You're little. You don't need this size."

"I do too," Bill said, lowering his own voice to try to meet her tone.

Rip saw his chance. "I think this one is just *my* size," he said, laughing as he began tugging on it from the other side.

Jon noticed the scuffle and stepped over to intervene. "Knock it off," he said in his no-nonsense voice. "If you tear these up, we won't have enough to go 'round." He called up the hill to his other counselor, "David, are you coming?"

"We'll be right behind you," David shouted. "I had a little trouble with the pump, but we're about done."

Corbin and Tommy came back down the hill weighted down with food and back packs. "We're ready to put in," she said.

"Okay," Jon spoke in his deepest voice so David's crew up the hill could hear as well as his own crew waiting just behind Corbin's raft. "Once more, here's the plan. The run will take about two hours. If you get to the take-out first, wait on the others. We'll all meet there, deflate the rafts, fix some lunch and then hike back to the vans. Be sure to strap down your food and packs tight so they won't pitch out. *And be careful in the class four water!* Remember, the Lord doesn't like to be tested, so don't do dumb stuff!"

"Yes, *sir*!" Rip said, pretending to cringe at Jon's authoritative tone.

"I don't mean to sound mean," Jon said with a smile, "but the Ocoee isn't just a thrill ride. It can be treacherous. You all had to be experienced rafters to qualify for this camp, but most of you haven't ridden the Ocoee. I want you to listen to your guides. Paddle exactly when and where they say, even if you think it's wrong."

Tommy noticed the writing on Corbin's tee shirt for the first time. It read, "Paddle or die!" Memory of Rip's comments yesterday sent a chill down his back. "Has anyone ever *really* died on this water?" he asked.

"Accidents can happen anywhere," Jon said. "Deaths have occurred in this river, but if we all pay attention to safety rules, we'll be fine. The water's shallow. Should you fall out, right yourself, float and reach for a rock or a limb and hold tight. Don't try to stand, the water will knock you down. Just hang on, and someone will pick you up. The main thing is not to panic."

"Let's go," Rip said. He had contained his hyperactivity about as long as possible.

"Right," Corbin said. "Into the water!"

Rip and Bill waded clumsily into the river, pulling

the cumbersome raft with them. Tommy followed close behind on one side, Vanessa on the other. They all scrambled over the sides and into the raft. Corbin brought up the rear, wading deepest into the river and jumping in as soon as they had cleared the bank enough to float free. "Grab your oars, and everyone be sure your feet are positioned to brace and balance you," she called out. Tommy snuck a glance at Vanessa's feet to be sure his own were correct. He had only rafted once, and wasn't sure he was positioned correctly. He was right; outside foot forward and snug against the raft, inside foot under his own seat. "Hang on to your oars, no matter what," she said. "If you fall out, your oar can help you keep from hitting the rocks too hard, and can help you float. Paddle left!!! Paddle right!!!"

Jon waited on the bank with his crew while David and his kids entered the water, then put in right behind them. "Get in the boat, Willy," he called out; the deputy was moving too deeply into the water to negotiate getting into the raft easily. Willy struggled over the side and fell in, making the raft bounce crazily. Jon followed the boat into the water, climbed in behind Willy, and repeated Corbin's orders to his own crew. "Paddle left!!! Paddle right!!!"

The Ocoee is a surprising river. Almost as soon as you leave the put-in, you face class four water in the area called "Grumpy." Corbin and her crew were in white water, moving rapidly among the rocks. The raft bounced and turned so fast it was almost impossible to shout paddle orders fast enough. The spray from water

51

hitting rocks blinded them, but her crew's instincts were good, and they worked together well. David's raft was close behind. Taking a short cut between rocks, it passed them, kids grinning widely as they flew by, paddling desperately. "Paddle!" Rip screamed. "Don't let them get ahead of us!"

"Don't worry," Corbin called out above the roar of the water. "We'll pass them at the next turn!"

The water, tinted golden from the color of the rocks, boiled and bubbled, swirled and whirl-pooled. As the boat turned in the spinning water, Corbin and her crew got a look at Jon's raft. Willy's oar hit a rock and flew up behind him, smacking into Jon's jaw! Stunned, Jon fell out of the raft, bobbing wildly in the churning water. His raft raced past him.

Corbin shouted to his panicking crew, "There's a big rock to your right! Use your oars to hold on to it."

They heard her over the river's roar and did as she directed, reaching out, barely grabbing the rock with their oars. The water pressed the raft against the rock as Jon, disoriented, struggled to stand in the racing water. He was immediately knocked down, and disappeared under the golden foam. Corbin saw Willy readying himself to jump in for a rescue. *"No, No!!"* she screamed as loud as she could. *"Don't go in! He'll be all right!"* She saw the indecision in Willy's face before the water swept them around a bend in the river, taking them out of sight of the drama upstream.

It was the first time Willy had been given orders by a girl, but he could see Corbin was right. He didn't know how to negotiate the water, and losing one more person wouldn't help Jon. Willy strained his eyes, trying to see under the water, praying to catch some sight of the big man he'd knocked out of the boat, maybe killed. Almost as soon as he went under, Jon realized where he was and tried to relax, but his body wouldn't respond to his commands. Instead, it fought against the raging river, which dragged him down and pounded him against the rocks at its bottom. Crazily, he thought of taking some deep breaths. The thought was so funny, he smiled, relaxed and rose straight to the surface. Still smiling, he floated until he banged into the raft and a grateful Willy pulled him in. "Are you okay?" he asked, voice filled with concern. The poor deputy's face was burning with shame.

"I'm fine," Jon replied, shaking the water out of his hair and ears. "Let's get this raft moving." The other boats were out of sight, a fact which worried Jon more than his aching jaw.

David and Corbin's rafts were waiting for their comrades in the slower water of "Gonzo Shoals." Jon was grateful to see them as his raft slid into the shoals' relative calm. In answer to their questioning stares, he called to them with a smile, "I'm fine, thanks be to God!" He unconsciously rubbed his swelling jaw. "Let's go for the 'Broken Nose.'"

The crews on all three rafts wore themselves out for the next forty minutes as they bobbed, raced, crashed and slid through quickly changing classes of white water. The ride was both exhilarating and frightening, like a very wet and unpredictable roller coaster. After "Gonzo Shoals," there was only one class one area where they could catch their breaths until tired and drained of adrenaline, they entered the calm water of the "Doldrums." Relieved and happy to be in quiet water, Tommy pulled in his oar and lay down across his seat. "What a beautiful sky," he said, staring upward. "I can't believe I'm still alive."

"Don't count your blessings too quick," Rip laughed. "The best is yet to come."

"Look!" Bill shouted, pointing to the river bank. "There's a bear."

Sure enough, standing on its hind legs a huge grizzly bear appeared to be waving a fish at them. It had come out to catch its dinner. The bear watched them closely, as if it found the people in the three boats as interesting as they found it. "Mr. Bear," Bill screamed. "Catch *me* a fish."

"That bear is probably wondering where we're camping tonight, so it can share some of our supper," Vanessa said. All her make-up had been washed away by the splashing, spraying water. She looked like some strange, lovely flower in her orange vest and blue helmet.

Tommy, after rising to look at the bear, lay back down and looked at the clouds. He began thinking of the murdered man. "Corbin," he said, "why do you think that man was killed?"

"I don't know," she answered, "but drugs are deadly, and people who get deeply into them usually die early one way or another."

"Why do people use drugs?" Rip wondered.

"Lots of people try them because someone they know invites them to. They don't want to seem scared or impolite. And most people don't believe they're going to get addicted; most people think they can stay in control."

Jo'Dee found this hard to understand. "We're taught all the time in school how bad drugs are, how addictive they are. Why would people think they wouldn't become addicts?"

"For the same reason people don't believe they'll get caught cheating on tests, or speeding in cars, or caught doing lots of illegal or immoral things. Some people think bad consequences are things that happen to other people, not them. Look at all the people you know who still smoke cigarettes, and kids start smoking every day even though everybody knows now how dangerous and addictive it is. Everyone believes they won't get cancer or heart disease. Everyone believes those things will happen to someone else. Then they get mad when they get cancer or have a heart attack, as if no one had warned them, when it says so right on the pack!"

Tommy sat up and looked at his aunt. "If I ever start to use drugs, make me stop," he said.

"I'll try," Corbin said. "But I might not be able to. The best thing is not to start at all, not to even *try* any of them. And if you start to smoke, I'll disown you!" The water around them was beginning to rush. Foam was forming. "We're in the 'Surprise' area," Corbin said. "Sit up and paddle. Paddle left!!! Paddle right!!!" Tommy could feel the jagged rocks under the raft as it raced over them and thought about the thin material in the boat's bottom, the only thing separating him from the furious water.

Chapter Six

White Water II

The glistening yellow rafts raced along on the raging yellow surf, crews struggling to negotiate rocks through the class four area at "Table Saw" and then making the sharp turn at "Diamond Slitter." Just as they reached the final Class IV water at "Hell's Hole," Corbin's boat spun completely around in the whirling water, crashing Tommy's oar against a log and snapping it out of his hands.

"Oh, no!" he cried, feeling helpless and frightened as he watched his broken oar bob away in the foam in front of their raft.

Rip saw the crippled oar float by and swung around to see who had lost it. "Tommy," he screamed, "you lost your oar!"

"Re-al-ly," Tommy screamed back, widening his eyes as if Rip were telling him something he didn't know. Hanging onto his seat, he turned around in the raft to try to see his aunt's face. He believed he would die on the spot if she criticized him.

"Don't worry," she said. Her grey eyes sparkled, turning blue in the glow from the bright helmet which outlined her wet face. "Debbie," she shouted over the water's roar, "Get Tommy an oar."

Catching her guide's words, Debbie felt under the seat and came up with the extra paddle. She handed it to Tommy with a grin. He just *knew* she was thinking he was a jerk for losing his, but he couldn't read it on her face.

"We're almost home," Corbin shouted. "Paddle right!!!" she called out. "Paddle left!!!."

The rafts flew in and out among the rocks, bobbing wildly. The cool water sprayed their hands and faces, which were burning in the sun. Suddenly David's boat was swamped by the rapids and began to sink. Luckily it had been pushed near the water's left bank. "Paddle right," he called out. "Get over to the edge so we can dump this water." "Paddle left!!! Paddle right!!!" Jon saw the swamped raft moving toward shore. David and his crew were deftly applying the oars, angling the raft so the racing water shoved it into the river bank. Fast as a crew in an auto racing pit stop they jumped out of the boat, lifted it and dumped the water, and were back in the river. Jon was happy for them to slip past him at the next bend.

"Paddle left!!! Paddle right!!!" were the only words heard until they slid into the relatively tranquil waters of the take-out area just north of "Hell's Hole." "Over there," Corbin said, pointing toward the river's edge. "There's where we go. Paddle left. Paddle right. Let's pull up on the bank. When we touch ground, Rip and Bill get out and hold the raft. Then Tommy and Vanessa get out and help pull us in."

The other exhausted crews sighted the take-out and moved their rafts toward the open docking area. After pulling up on the river bank, Corbin's kids took off their helmets and life jackets and lay down on the cool, damp ground. Tommy lay face down, and felt like kissing the rocky soil under him. David's raft came in a close second, followed by Jon and his crew. Just as the second raft touched the river bank, Corbin was surprised to see the sheriff walking toward them from the woods. "I'm sure glad to see y'all," he said, smiling and tipping his Stetson. He went on to the river bank where Jon's raft was coming in and caught the line Willy threw him.

"Hi," Jon said. "What brings you way out here?" The crew piled out of the raft and helped the sheriff drag it up on the bank. The reclining kids reluctantly got up to see what was going on. Willy hurried over to stand by his boss's side.

"I've got the Explorer up on the trail. I came out to see if you'd let Corbin and Tommy come into town with me an' Willy to look at some folks in a line-up. We rounded up some suspects. May not have the right man yet, but we need to begin the process of elimination."

"Did you arrest someone?" Tommy asked, suddenly filled with energy.

"Not exactly," the sheriff drawled. "We know most of the dope dealers around the campus, and we love to drag them in any chance we get. But it's possible we've got your man, so it's worth takin' a look-see."

"We've had a tough morning," Jon said. "Can't we wait till we have some lunch and rest a little? You're welcome to eat with us."

"It'd be quicker if I got the kids some lunch in town," Sheriff Crockett answered. "If it's okay with you, we'll do that, then we can get 'em back to the campsite before dark. I can't hold these Bozos too long. They holler to their sleazy lawyer, and he comes and gets 'em released."

Jon looked questioningly at Corbin and Tommy, who eagerly nodded their heads. The plan was fine with them. Corbin was only mildly resentful over being called a "kid."

"Okay," Jon said. "I guess they can go. You know where the campsite is. What'll you do if we're not back there yet?"

"We'll just wait for you. But you'll prob'ly beat us there. If they don't recognize anyone in the line up, we'll leave Willy with you again tonight."

"What about dry clothes?" Jon asked.

"We'll be fine," Corbin said. "These will dry out in no time. Just let me get my pack out of the raft. Tommy, get whatever you need to carry to town."

Tommy was anxious to go with the sheriff. "I don't

need anything," he said.

"Get your pack," Corbin ordered. "You need your comb. Your hair is standing straight up."

"Good grief," he complained. "You sound like my mother!" Reluctantly Tommy did as he was told while Willy searched through the packs on Jon's raft until he found his own. Then the four walked up the hill and were lost in the trees. The rest of the campers watched them until Bill chirped "Let's eat!"

Amazingly, Corbin went to sleep as they bounced over the rough mountain trail in the Explorer. Two hours of intense concentration and exertion had exhausted her. But Tommy was wired; he talked the sheriff's ears off.

"What did they find out about the tire tracks?" he asked. "Were they able to tell what kind of car the man drove?"

"They got some good prints," the sheriff answered. "The tire was cut some on one side; there's a pretty distinctive mark on it. Of course we don't know for sure it was the car our man was driving, but it probably was. He sure didn't carry the body there on foot. When we get a case built, the print'll help nail the top on it."

"Cool," Tommy said, "but what kind of car was it, can they tell from the kind of tire it was?"

"That kind of tire's usually on a sports utility vehicle like a Blazer or Explorer," the sheriff said thoughtfully. Personally, he loved his own vehicle, and hated to think a murderer could like the same kind of car he drove. He'd always thought of murderers as though they were completely alien, with nothing at all in common with him.

Tommy's mind was racing on, remembering that last night someone mentioned the medical examiner would do an autopsy. "Did the medical examiner do the autopsy," he asked. "What did he find?"

"Well, he found some interestin' things. The man who went over the falls wasn't killed then. He was already dead. He was killed earlier."

"How could he tell that?" Tommy asked. Curious and bright, he usually understood complicated things if they were explained to him.

"I don't understand all the details," the sheriff admitted reluctantly. "But it has somethin' to do with the brusin', it's different when blood's flowin' and when it isn't."

"Oh," Tommy said. "That makes sense. Then what do they think killed him?"

"The M.E. found a wound at the base of his skull that he thinks did the deed. And it wasn't made by anything sharp like rocks. It was a blunt object."

Tommy couldn't believe it. Just like in the movies, the man was killed by a blunt instrument! "Was there anything else? Could they tell when he was killed?"

"Well," the sheriff said, "they couldn't tell when he was killed too accurately because of him lying in the cool water. But there was another interestin' thing. He had a burn on his face. The M.E. said it looked like it had been made by an iron."

Tired as he was, this got even Willy's attention. "An iron?" he asked, sitting up and turning toward his boss. "What kind of an iron?"

"Just a plain ole iron, I guess," the sheriff said. "Like you iron clothes with. He said that was the shape of the burn. And it was made before he was killed, but not long before he was killed. It hadn't started to heal!"

"What do you think that means?" Tommy asked. This was getting more and more puzzling.

"I don't know," the sheriff said. "I can't picture dope dealers usin' ironing boards. But we'll go on into town and let you kids see this lineup, anyways. It might at least help you remember somethin'."

The Explorer bumped along, entering what the faculty and students called the "domain." Now they were on Ocoee University property. Through the trees, Tommy could see buildings ahead. He strained his eyes, trying to spot the fifty-to-sixty-foot high cliffs where the campers were to rock climb and rappel in a couple of days. Corbin had told him they were down a short road on the edge of the campus. Of all the things they were going to do, the only ones which frightened Tommy were climbing and rappelling. He'd never had the chance to do them before; he didn't believe he could do them now because of his fear of heights. And he dreaded looking like a geek.

"Are the cliffs we're going to rappel on near here?" he asked softly, not wanting to wake Corbin and have her sense his anxiety.

"Naw," the sheriff said. "The place where the kids rappel is further across the campus, over beyond the chapel."

"Oh," Tommy said. His stomach growled, and his thoughts changed to food. "Where do we eat?" he asked.

"Right here," the sheriff said, pulling up by some shops and businesses.

"Wake up," Tommy said, playfully punching his aunt in the side. "Lunch is served!"

CHAPTER SEVEN

The Killer

Although long past college age, the sheriff knew where Corbin and Tommy would want to eat. On the Ocoee University campus, there was a place where students gathered which was informal to say the least. Called simply "The Hangout," it was an old wooden building with no paint on the walls and no covering on the plain wooden floors. In fact, almost everything was made of wood. The tables and booths were ancient, as were the chairs and the long counter where the students were served. Although the day was bright, The Hangout was dark; tables were lit with candles and there were dim lights above the crowded counter where Corbin, Tommy, Willy and the sheriff stepped up to place their orders.

The menu was hand written in huge chalk letters on a long blackboard on the back wall and offered everything from huge, greasy cheeseburgers and fries to health food! Great jars of dill pickles and other things not so familiar to Corbin sat on the counter. The Hangout employed students, who raced around taking orders and bringing out plates of food from the kitchen. The sheriff and his little group decided to play it safe; they all ordered cheeseburgers, fries and Cokes, then moved toward the back where they spied an empty booth.

Corbin told the others she would have to make a "pit stop" before she ate. The sheriff pointed her in the right direction, toward the front near the door to the kitchen. As soon as Corbin turned around, the guys grabbed their burgers and started to eat.

Corbin was grateful to have a few minutes alone; she stopped in front of the mirror to comb her hair and consider her reflection before she left the ladies' room. Her face was really burned. She hoped it wouldn't blister. Speaking of blisters, her fingers were itching. She looked at them. Sure enough, besides the red sunburn, little red bumps were showing. "Oh, no!" she thought. "I'll have to get the sheriff to take me to a drug store and get some poison ivy medicine. I don't want this stuff to spread." She put her comb away in her pack and, feeling hunger pangs, intended to go out and head straight for their booth. But as she left the ladies' room, bright light coming through The Hangout's front door attracted her attention. There, silhouetted in the door, stood the man she had seen at the top of the falls. It was the murderer!

She could only see his outline at first, but she was sure it was him. As her eyes became more accustomed to the light, she saw that he had brown hair, pulled back in what was probably a pony tail. She could just make out his features; high cheek bones and a long nose. He was staring into the restaurant. Corbin followed his line of sight to the booth where the sheriff and the others sat. Only the sheriff and Willy were visible, leaning toward each other across the table. Tommy sat next to the sheriff, hidden by the Stetson the sheriff had neglected to remove. She looked back to the man in the door. He was gone! He must have seen the sheriff and bolted.

Corbin ran to go the booth. "He was here," she cried. "He was over there in the door."

"Wait a minute," Sheriff Crockett drawled. "Who was here?"

"The killer! The man at the falls! He was right here, right in the door just a second ago. I think he saw you and left."

"Which way did he go?" Willy asked.

"I don't know. He was right there. I turned to see where he was looking. When I turned back he was gone."

The sheriff was on his feet. "Let's see if we can spot him. Come on!"

The four raced for the door, food forgotten. The student at the cash register followed after them a few steps, but realizing it was the sheriff who had dashed out without paying the bill, he let them go. Outside, Corbin looked right and left, shading her eyes with her hand, scanning the narrow street. There was no sign of him. And there were lots of doors available for him to duck into. She turned to the sheriff. "What now?"

"Now," he said, "we finish our lunch. Willy, get the car phone and tell the guys at the office to let those men go we had for the lineup. No need to keep them waiting there for nothing."

"Yes'r," Willy responded, jogging across the street to the Explorer. He sometimes wished he were the boss, especially at times like this when his lunch was getting colder and colder.

The sheriff swung the heavy door to The Hangout open and shouted at the student who was about to clean up their table, "Don't touch that food! We're not through." The group moved back to their booth and took their seats. "You're sure it was the same man?" Sheriff Crockett asked Corbin.

"Oh, yes. I'm sure. I thought I wouldn't remember enough to recognize him. But when I saw him outlined by the light in the door, I knew him. His silhouette must be burned into my brain. And now I know what the rest of him looks like."

"What *does* he look like?" Tommy asked.

Corbin described the man while she scooted over so Willy could join them. "What do we do now?" she asked again, feeling like a broken record. Although her burger was cold, she was starving and it was delicious.

She drank her Coke as if she were dying of thirst.

"I've been thinking," the sheriff said. "If he's a student, his picture might be in the yearbook. But if he's a freshman it won't. How old did he look?"

"He looked older than my friends and I," Corbin said. "I'd guess he's at least a junior if he's a student."

"Then we go to the campus administration office and get them to let you look at the yearbook. We'll start there. If you don't find him, we'll go to the art department and see if anybody there can draw him for us. Our little sheriff's department isn't fancy enough to have an artist, but somebody here at the university may be able to help us out."

"Why do you think he ran?" Tommy asked. "Do you think he saw me and recognized me from the falls?"

"I don't think so," Corbin said. "I couldn't see you behind the sheriff's hat, and I don't think he could either."

Sheriff Crockett took off his Stetson to scratch his forehead. "It was prob'ly just a guilty conscience. He's prob'ly just scared of the law. An' he's right to be scared. We're goin' to find him, and we're goin' to nail him for murder. Are you about through, little lady?"

"Just a couple more bites," Corbin said, smiling through her mouth full of fries. She had decided earlier not to be angry over the sheriff's lack of feminine political correctness.

Sheriff Crockett heaved his small frame up from the booth as though he weighed a ton. Strangely, he moved like a big man. "I'm goin' to go on over and pay the kid. Don't worry," he said as he noticed Corbin reaching for her pack. "The meal's on the department."

"Thanks," Tommy said, proud that he was a valuable enough witness to have the sheriff pay for his meal. He picked up his pack and followed the small man toward the front, unconsciously mimicking his swagger.

The university campus was beautiful. It was old, and although many buildings had been built later, it was founded before the Civil War. The style was greystone English gothic. If it hadn't been for the blue-jean clad students, it might have been a campus in England instead of east Tennessee.

The university administration building was nearby; it didn't take long for the little group to arrive there. It was huge. Corbin had always felt administration buildings were meant to look scary so people wouldn't go there often and bother the staff. The first staff person they saw suggested they look in the library until the sheriff explained that if they identified the man, they would need administrative staff's help to locate him on campus. Then the woman was very nice and helpful, finding the yearbooks for them after searching through several offices. The books were big. She showed Corbin and Tommy an empty desk where they could sit and pore over the pictures.

Time went by. The sheriff and Willy paced the floor. Waiting wasn't what they did best. Occasionally one or the other would go over to the desk and ask, "Have you found him yet?" Inevitably Corbin would answer,

"No." They finally reached the end of the last yearbook. He wasn't there.

"Does this mean he isn't a student," Tommy asked, disappointed and afraid now they wouldn't be able to catch the man.

"Not necessarily," Corbin answered. "Lots of students don't get their pictures in the yearbook for one reason or another."

"She's right," the sheriff said. "Now we go to the art department and see if we can get somebody there to draw our suspect."

"Where's the art department?" Tommy asked.

"I know where it is," Sheriff Crockett answered, reaching out and automatically rubbing down Tommy's cowlick. He had sons of his own. "The university's part of my territory. It's my job to know where everything is."

Corbin noticed the sheriff's hand as he rubbed Tommy's head. Red blisters were forming between the fingers. "You've got it, too," she said.

"Got what?" he asked, confused.

"Poison ivy," she said, pointing to his fingers.

"Oh, good golly!" he said, looking at his hand.

"Can we stop at a drug store and get something for it? We don't want it to spread." Corbin had it on her face as a child and knew what kind of damage it could do.

"Sure," he said. "Let's go."

The group climbed back into the Explorer and after circling back to the business district for Ivyrest, they located the art department. The sheriff quickly found a faculty member, easy to spot in a crumpled linen jacket and jeans, and explained their situation. The professor was cordial and interested. He took them to a studio on the building's top floor where daylight streamed through skylights in the high ceiling, and introduced them to Dr. Snow.

"This is Sheriff Crockett, his deputy, Corbin and Tommy," he said, "and they need your help."

Corbin was impressed that the professor remembered their names. "We're looking for a man who may have committed a murder," she said. "I saw the man, and I can tell you what he looks like if you'll draw him."

Dr. Snow was a greying, middle-aged woman with a wrinkled, interesting face. She reminded Corbin of her mom. "I've never done any forensic work," she said, "but I'll be glad to try. You say this man is a murderer? Whom did he kill?"

"He killed a drug dealer, mam," Sheriff Crockett said. "Not much of a loss, but he needs to be brought to justice."

"I should hope so!" Dr. Snow said. "How did the kids become involved?"

"We're camping at Rainbow Falls. We were at the bottom of the falls when this guy threw the drug dealer's body over. It fell right in the pool in front of us," Tommy said.

"We're kind of in a hurry, mam," the sheriff interrupted, somewhat impatiently. "We need to get this picture out to the deputies as soon as we can, so we can catch this Bozo. Corbin saw the man just a little while ago. He's prob'ly still on the campus."

"Of course," Dr. Snow said, slightly embarrassed. "I'm sorry. We don't get many murderers among our student body, thank goodness. Tell me, Corbin. What did the man look like?"

Dr. Snow found a sketch pad and began to draw while Corbin carefully described him. Watching the drawing progress, Corbin occasionally asked her to erase and redraw a line. Soon, she was more than satisfied. Dr. Snow had drawn the man! "Yes!," Corbin said. "It's almost as good as a photograph."

"Yes," Tommy agreed, wanting to be part of the action. "That's him."

"We're mighty grateful, mam," Sheriff Crockett said, remembering his manners.

"I'm happy to help," Dr. Snow smiled. "I hope I deserve a call when you catch him."

"For sure," Corbin said. "You'll be one of the first to know we've got him. And it'll be all because of your picture."

They took the sketch and hurried down the hall, down the stairs, and out the door. They jumped in the Explorer and drove straight to the sheriff's office on the edge of town. Corbin, Tommy and Willy were exhausted. They dropped into chairs scattered about the office, while the sheriff barked orders to other deputies concerning the photocopying of the sketch and its distribution. "Get this out to every man and woman in the department, and to every campus cop. This man is wanted for murder. Call me any time of the day or night if he's spotted. Understood?"

Corbin realized in the excitement they'd forgotten their friends in the woods. "It's getting late," she said to anyone who might be listening. "We should get on back to go the campground. I don't want Jon and the others to go worry about us."

Tommy wasn't so anxious to go. He'd never been inside the workings of a real sheriff's Department before. "Can't we stay awhile and see if they get him?" he asked, not quite begging.

"It may take awhile before we catch him," Willy said.

"Before *we* catch him?" Sheriff Crockett said to his deputy. "You have to go back and stay with the kids."

"But you need me here," Willy whined; he wasn't ashamed to beg.

"I need you where I say I need you," the sheriff said. "You're going back to Rainbow Falls. This guy may have hidden in a doorway and spotted us coming out of The Hangout. I need you there now more than ever."

Willy smiled at Corbin and Tommy, showing he meant no hard feelings. "Let's go," he said.

It was supper time when they got back to the campsite. The sheriff was grateful for Jon's invitation to stay and eat. He brought everyone up to date and showed them the picture Dr. Snow had drawn. Nothing exciting had happened to the campers. The sheriff left early. Prayers that night were mostly about gratitude for the campers' safety on the river and for getting a picture of the killer out into the community. Jon took the opportunity to remind the group that vengeance belongs to the Lord; they shouldn't become too excited about the manhunt going on on campus. The weary campers turned in. Everyone wanted a good night's sleep and an early start the next morning.

CHAPTER EIGHT

An Uninvited Guest

Although exhausted, Willy, Tommy and Corbin lay awake in their tents for what seemed like hours. Sometime in the middle of the night, just as Corbin fell asleep, a sound outside the tent startled her. Inside her sleeping bag she froze with fear. "It's the murderer," she thought. "He followed us, and he's outside my tent trying to kill me." Her mind raced, thinking of what to do. Should she call out for help? Or should she first try to see what was going on out there? Somewhat relieved to feel reason taking over, she decided the latter was the best course. Making almost no noise, she slid far enough out of her bag to lift the canvas at the back of the tent and peek out. At first she saw only darkness, then a moving, blacker outline emerged. It was too large

and not the right shape for a man. "Good grief!" she thought, "It's the bear!"

Quickly she dropped the canvas, not wanting the bear to catch her scent. "He's after our food," she thought, "and he's big, at least six feet tall, so he's old enough to be familiar with people and campsites." Corbin strained her ears, listening intently, trying to make out the bear's movements. She heard a clang as a metal trash can hit the ground. "He's trying to get at our garbage," she realized. There was a receptacle just behind her tent. Mentally, she went over the location of the other tents, remembering who was in them. She thought of Willy and his gun, but she didn't want the animal hurt if it wasn't necessary. Since the bear was occupied with the trash can, she decided she could make it to Jon's tent without attracting its attention.

Ever so slowly and quietly, she slipped out of her sleeping bag and lifted the tent flap. Her eyes were accommodated to the dark and the sky was filled with stars; she could see fairly well. Jon's tent lay directly in front of her, with Tommy's in between. She could still hear the bear struggling to get the cover off the metal receptacle, so she had her chance. She crept silently out into the night, grateful for the damp mulch which kept her movements almost noiseless.

Jon was dreaming of falling out of an airplane without a parachute. He fell effortlessly through the air, spinning and diving, occasionally spreading his arms and gliding like a great bird. Just as he was about to hit ground, he felt someone touch his shoulder. Looking blindly up into the dark tent, he was surprised to hear Corbin's voice in his ear, "There's a bear in back of my tent."

Unzipping his bag, he sat straight up. "You're not kidding?" he asked groggily.

"I'm not kidding," she said. "What do we do?"

Jon's faculties were arranging themselves. He immediately sized up the situation and recalled the standard bear-in-the-campsite strategy. "We make noise," he whispered. "Lots of noise. I'll get over by the fire where the pots and pans are, and bang them together and holler as loud as I can. You scoot over to the van and blow the horn and flash the lights." He groped around the tent for his keys. "The sound and lights'll drive him back into the woods," he said with more assurance than he felt.

Corbin looked puzzled. "But the kids'll come running out to see what's going on" she whispered back.

"It won't matter. They'll come toward us, the bear will go in the opposite direction. It's the safest way to handle it for everyone, including our furry visitor." Jon pulled himself the rest of the way out of the bag. "Let's get our bearings—ha ha—then make a dash for it. You go straight to the van. Start blowing the horn and flashing the lights as soon as you get in."

"Okay," Corbin said, taking a deep breath. "Let's go!"

Jon got to the fire site before Corbin got to the van. He picked up a heavy iron skillet and pan. Basically a quiet man, unused to creating a commotion, Jon at first hesitated to bang metal on metal and scream. But when he heard Corbin blow the horn and flash the lights, he found his courage and began to make a deafening clang with the utensils, while shouting at the top of his deep voice.

The noise brought everyone scurrying out of their tents, some in Jon's direction, some toward the van. Everyone, that is, except the bear, who slid silently into the blackness of the forest. Jon and Corbin continued the sound and light show for a good five minutes, not stopping to answer the frightened campers' questions.

Still banging the pans and shouting, Jon moved through the campsite to the back of Corbin's tent. Beginning to enjoy making a racket (his parents had never let him make much noise), he was almost sorry to see that the bear had left. But the evidence of its presence was plain. The metal garbage receptacle was on its side, dented from the powerful animal's efforts to open it. "It's okay," Jon called out. "It's gone."

Corbin turned the headlights off and climbed out of the van, running to join Jon behind her tent. The rest of the campers weren't sure where to go, so they instinctively gathered at the fire site, slightly disoriented and afraid in the dark chilly night. Willy suddenly noticed he'd forgotten his gun; in the excitement he'd left it in the holster in the tent!

Corbin and Jon were satisfied the bear had high-tailed it deep into the forest, scared enough not to return. Coming around her tent, they saw everyone hovering around the fire site.

"I'll bet it was a bear!" Rip called out.

"You're right," Jon said. "But it's long gone into the woods, the devil scared out of it."

"How big was it?" Bill wanted to know.

"Did you see it, Corbin?" Calvin asked.

"I saw it," she said. "And it was big, bigger than Jon!"

"Wow," Debbie said. "Will it come back? Doesn't it want food?"

"It wants food, all right," Jon said, "but I don't think it's coming back."

"But what if it does?" Vanessa asked, a slight catch in her voice.

"We'll need to stand guard," Willy said. Somehow he felt he should have been the one to deal with the bear. After all, he was here to protect everyone; instead he'd come out without his gun. "I'll keep watch," he offered.

"You're right," Jon said. "We should have guards, but we need more than one, and we should do shifts. If we don't everyone'll be too tired to go caving."

"Then I'll take the first shift," Willy said. "Who's going to keep watch with me?"

"I'd like to," Jo'Dee said. She really enjoyed being up at night, but seldom got the chance.

"Fine," Jon said. "You two take the first watch. Wake David up in four hours to relieve you. Who's going to watch with David?"

"I will," Bill said before anyone else could respond.

"Fine," Jon said. "Everybody give me a hand

getting the fire started.

The campers threw fat wood and logs over the cold ashes; soon a cheery blaze was throwing long, dancing shadows against the trees. In spite of the excitement, everyone was so tired they all shuffled back to their tents and went immediately to sleep. Willy went to his tent to retrieve his gun, then came back to sit near the fire by Jo'Dee.

At first the two watchers talked quietly about the day's strange events. But tired, they soon leaned back against their respective trees to think their own, private thoughts. The night was almost completely silent; the animals and insects who sang in the evening had finished their humming and chirping. Jo'Dee didn't notice that Willy had fallen asleep until she heard him begin to snore softly. Her dad called her a "first born person," meaning she was very comfortable with herself and her place in the world. And tonight she was just as happy to be alone, watching the dancing flames, imagining seeing scenes, animals and people in them. When their four hours were up, she made noise with the logs on the fire, gently waking Willy without his knowing she knew he was sleeping.

"Well," she said, "that sure went fast. It's time to wake up David and Bill."

Willy stretched his legs out in front of him, getting the blood flowing before he tried to stand up. "You're right," he said. "It sure went fast. I'll get David." He dragged himself to his feet, which were still asleep in his boots. Grateful to feel the feeling returning, he lumbered over to David's tent and quietly called to him, not wanting to disturb the other campers.

David was sleeping lightly and woke easily. He was the type of person who could go for days on little sleep. He came out of his tent quickly, and went over to wake Bill.

Bill was a different sort of animal. He slept heavily; his mom threatened to throw him, mattress and all, out of bed and onto the floor some school mornings. Getting no response from his call, David went into the tent to wake him. "Come on, guy," David said. "You volunteered, now you've got to do the duty!" He shook Bill's shoulder to get his attention.

"Okay, okay," Bill grumped. "I'm coming." He stuck his tousled blond head out of the bag, remembering why he was being waked up in the middle of the night. He was on the bear watch! Wide awake now, he moved quickly out of the tent and stood at David's side.

"Good night," David called quietly to Jo'Dee and Willy.

"Good night," Jo'Dee said, reluctantly going to her tent. She would have liked to volunteer for another watch, but seeing how eager Bill was, she didn't mention it.

"G'night," Willy waved, gratefully going into his tent and falling asleep almost before he got inside his bag.

David went over and sat by the fire. It needed feeding, but he felt too lazy to pull over the logs just yet. Bill sat down next to him and immediately realized his stomach was growling. "I'm hungry," he said.

"The food's put up," David said. "It's all over in Jon's van."

"That's OK," Bill said. "Maybe Corbin forgot to lock it. I'm going to go over and see."

"Oh, all right," David said, "if you're that hungry. Take my flashlight, and try not to make much noise closing the door. Don't wake everybody up!"

Bill ran lightly toward the van, shining the powerful light in front of him. He was right! In the excitement, Corbin had left the door unlocked. He climbed in, moved to the back, and rummaged through the food until he found chips. Picking up a paper bag to put everything in, he flashed the light inside the cooler and found the kind of soda he liked. His mother's voice sounded in his head: "Remember your manners." Picking out a drink for David, he climbed out of the van.

He looked for the glow of the fire, but couldn't see it. It must have burned down too low. The stars above him in the road's clearing were bright and beautiful. He decided not to use the flash on the way back. He didn't want it accidentally to shine into a tent on a sleeping camper's face. Coming around in front of Calvin's tent, he caught sight of the fire's glowing embers. A small flame feebly illuminated David as he sat, chin in hands, staring straight ahead. But he wasn't alone. The bear was back! Bill saw its deep black outline, standing up on its hind legs, towering over David's head. It's eyes glowed and its bright, white teeth gleamed in the dim firelight. And Corbin was right! It was *huge!*

This was Bill's first crisis, and he rose to the occasion. He swung the huge flashlight up in front of him, and screaming, ran straight toward the bear.

David reacted quickly. As soon as he saw Bill running toward him, screaming, he knew what it meant. He dove across the fire, and landing on his feet on the other side, he spun around, yelling at the bear at the top of his lungs. The noise brought the other campers out; they all began to scream and holler at the bear.

Bewildered and disappointed, the bear turned and sprinted for the woods. Black as a starless night, the animal disappeared so quickly Bill almost wondered if he had really seen it. "Go on," Bill screamed. "And don't come back!"

"Good grief," Jon said after he was certain the bear had again exited, "are we going to get any sleep at all tonight?"

"I'll bet that's all we'll see of him," David laughed. "I think we really scared him this time."

"That's what we thought last time," Corbin said, yawning with her hand covering her mouth.

"Come on," Jon said. "Everybody back in bed. It'll be dawn before we know it." They dragged themselves back into their tents.

David threw logs on the embers, while Bill discovered he still had hold of the bag with the sodas and chips. They took up their seats by the fire. "Want a soda," Bill asked, handing the cold can out to David, who took it gratefully. Apparently running off a bear made one thirsty.

"Want some chips?" Bill asked.

"I sure do," David said, smiling at the young man. "Do you know how brave you are? You saved my life; that bear could have had me for sure."

"Oh," Bill said, shyly, his crackly voice breaking even more than usual, "I doubt it. He just wanted our left-overs."

"Anyway, I'm grateful to you. And you *are* very brave." David put out his hand for Bill to high-five. Bill beamed, cheeks red in the fire's rosy glow.

CHAPTER NINE

The Forest

In spite of the night's interruptions and vigils, the campers rose at daybreak, and after giving thanks to God for a quick breakfast, they cleaned up, packed up, and were in the vans again. They drove onto the campus, past the chapel and down the dirt road which began at the top of the bluffs where the campers were to rappel the next day. The narrow road ran down through a pass in the bluffs, then descended to run along the edge of the old growth forest. Just out of sight of the rocky bluffs, Jon pulled the lead van off the road. David's van pulled off behind him. There were several wild caves on the domain, the one they were headed for was called Wagon Cover. Its huge opening looked like the cover on a Conestoga wagon, only tremendously larger. It was located at the bottom of a thousand-foot-deep gorge. But before they could begin the decent into the gorge, the campers had to hike two miles through primeval woods. They parked the vehicles as close to the trail as possible; the counselors knew how tired they would all be when they got back.

The forest was amazingly beautiful; everyone fell silent as they entered it, as if it were a holy place. It had been undisturbed for centuries. Even the least religious of the kids couldn't help feeling God's presence there in his creation. Sixty feet above them, branches of ancient yellow poplars and white oaks intertwined, dancing together in the light wind. Rustling leaves of hickory, ash and sugar maple provided soft music. The trees' canopy was so dense little sunlight made its way through, but what did produced bright flashes of gold. A variety of birds called out to one another, some singing, some seeming to be in a constant argument, fussing and flying high overhead among the branches, paying no notice to the campers passing underneath.

Jon led the pack, and as they hiked deeper into the woods, remembered to remind everyone to stay on the path. "Don't stray off," he called out. "The woods look inviting, but they're not safe. Remember the bear we saw? It has relatives."

Watching her step among the large roots to keep from tripping, Corbin marched along near the middle of the group. Damp, dead leaves beneath her feet sighed softly as she stepped on them, intensifying the rich earthy odor of the forest. Although she loved the woods, she didn't like the long hike with its difficult climb down into and then, later, up out of the gorge. To take her mind off it, she thought of the word "spelunk," the fancy word for caving, and wondered who thought it up. Spelunking was one of her favorite sports; wild caves were dangerous and exciting, even more so than white water rafting. She hadn't told Tommy this; wild caving was something he hadn't done yet and she didn't want to frighten him.

Because of the hike and climb everyone packed light; each carried sandwiches, cookies, helmets, drinks and flashlights. The counselors carried extra batteries; having your light go out in a wild cave is not good! Jon also carried rope and a first aid kit, just in case. The plan was to leave the packs outside the cave, explore inside, then eat when they came out. Packs would be left behind to give the spelunkers more mobility in scooting under rocks and through narrow crevices inside the cave. They didn't expect human predators to steal their packs on the campus domain, and bears wouldn't be able to smell the food inside.

Rip was getting both tired and bored with the hike, seeing nothing much but plants and birds. "When do we get there?" he called out to no one in particular.

David was behind him. "We're almost to the gorge," he answered. "You'd better save your breath, you're going to need it!"

Before Rip could think of a wisecrack answer, a shriek split the serenity of the woods. The campers stopped in their tracks and looked around. At first they couldn't tell whether it was a wildcat or a human voice. The voice screamed again. It was human, and it came from behind them. Everyone turned and ran toward the sound.

"*Stop!*" Jon ordered, halting them with his commanding voice. "Get back on the trail and stay there!"

"Where is it? Who is it?" Corbin asked.

David went into the woods, shooing the kids back onto the path. "Over here," he shouted. "It's Debbie." He knew she had been the last in line and now she was missing. Corbin left the trail and followed him; Jon and Willy were close behind her.

Not far off, they could hear Debbie's terrified voice. "Help," she cried, "Somebody help me!"

Walking carefully, they watched their steps and moved closer to the place where her voice seemed to rise up out of the ground. "Oh, no!" Jon whispered. "She's fallen through a sinkhole."

"Hold on," David hollered down to her. "Don't move around. Just be still and we'll get you out."

"How deep do you think she is?" Corbin wondered.

"Let's ask," Jon said. "Debbie," he called out to her, feeling somewhat silly, looking like he was talking to no one. But he didn't want her to hear fear in his voice. "Do you know how deep you are?"

"Not very, I think," the strained voice responded as she tried to see daylight above her. The ground had fallen in and over her when it gave way, so she had been afraid to move, even before she was told not to. Intuition told her that movement might plunge her deeper into the earth. Now that she knew she was heard, fear was joined by embarrassment at having to be rescued. She felt so dumb! Trying to regain some composure before continuing her answer she said, "I think I only fell a few feet."

"What do we do?" Willy asked, feeling helpless and useless. This was a situation where his gun wouldn't help.

"We've got to be careful," Corbin said. "Some sink holes open into caves, and can go down to China. There are lots of them in these woods. We've got to try to keep her from falling in any deeper, but it won't help if *we* fall in one."

Jon looked at the two men standing beside him and at Corbin. "You're the lightest," he said.

"Okay," she sighed. "I'll go. I'm going to try and step over to that little tree and tie myself to it. You brought the rope didn't you?"

Jon pulled the long, coiled rope out of his bag. "Here you go," he said, giving her the coils and holding onto one end himself. "I'll hold onto it until you get to the tree. I hope there's a rock over there big enough to sink the rope."

"There'll have to be, won't there?" Corbin said. She prayed for help, held her breath and stepped as lightly as possible over to the little tree she hoped would keep her out of Debbie's and any other nearby sinkhole. Reaching the sapling and finding herself standing on firm ground, she sighed in relief. She tied one end of the rope around the tree, pulled the other end up as Jon released it, then ran the rope across her shoulders and over her arm to free her hands. Just as she expected, God was with her. A big rock lay partially hidden under the dead leaves, just within reach. She unwound the rest of the rope and tied the rock to the end. If Debbie stayed still, they might just make it, she thought. She shot her fellow counselors an apprehensive thumbs up.

"Don't worry," David reassured her. "It'll work. It'll be all right."

Leaning into the rope, she inched her way toward the sinkhole, taking baby steps in her big boots. "Debbie," she called in the most comforting voice possible under the circumstances, "Don't move. Be very still. I'm almost there."

Buried beneath the earth, Debbie wasn't totally reassured. Dirt was in her eyes and mouth, and she was beginning to hyperventilate. She turned her face toward the narrow opening above her. "Please hurry," she said between gulps of air. Suddenly she lost her balance and stepped to the side. The earth fell away beneath her foot, and she began to fall. "Lord, help me" her mind cried out, but a scream came from her throat. She plunged down another five feet before the narrow walls of rock stopped her. Her upper body was resting against the rock chimney, her feet dangled in the air above heaven knew what.

"Debbie," Corbin called out, now not even trying to hide the concern in her voice; she had heard dirt sliding and Debbie's scream. "Are you there, are you all right?"

Hanging between the rocks, Debbie at first thought she couldn't answer. There seemed to be no air in her lungs. But she was tough; tougher than she looked, and she wanted to get out. She drew in her breath and called up, "I'm okay. I fell some more." She pressed her arms against the rock on each side and lifted herself slightly to breathe deeper.

"Don't move," Corbin called down to her. "Please don't move anymore."

"Don't worry," Debbie said, almost laughing at the unintentional humor in Corbin's command. "I couldn't move if I wanted to. I'm stuck between the rocks."

"Thank goodness," Corbin said. "I'm going to drop a rope with a rock tied to it down to you. Can you put your hands over your head so it won't hit you?"

"Sure," Debbie answered. Adrenaline had been pumping so hard for so long, she was beginning to feel as if she could do anything.

Corbin lowered the rock with the rope attached down the opening in the earth. From above, it was impossible to tell how deep the sinkhole might be. It could end just below her or go down for a thousand feet to the bottom of the gorge, ending somewhere far inside Wagon Top Cave. Corbin said a prayer of gratitude that Debbie was caught by the rocks, and let out a few more feet of rope. "Have you got it yet?"

I've *got* it!" Debbie cried in disbelief, as the heavy rock fell into her open hands.

"Okay, Just hold on a minute." Corbin made the rope firm around her shoulder and tightened the slack across her body. "Now see if you can pull yourself up some. Don't try to move fast. Just see if you can come up a little."

Corbin felt the rope tighten against her body and saw the ground around the sink hole holding firm. "How're you doin'?" she called down?

"I'm moving up some," Debbie said, almost too softly to hear.

"The earth is firm in front of me," Corbin said. "Face toward my voice. Push on the rock walls with your arms and feet to help yourself up."

Debbie pressed her arms against the cool earth around her. "It's solid," came the joyful voice out of the hole.

Corbin was thankful for the strong fibers that held the weight of the tiny young woman as she inched her way out of the sinkhole. She tried not to notice that the rough rope against her fingers was popping the poison ivy blisters. "Then come on up," she said. "But go slow; take your time."

Debbie's red head appeared, covered with the mulch of last fall's leaves. As the rest of her body came into view, it was all the other counselors and Willy could do not to run up and pull her out. They had to watch as she struggled on her own, pulling herself hand over hand, boots straining against the black earth until Corbin grabbed her by the wrist.

"What some people will do for attention!" Corbin laughed, teasing her younger friend and brushing dirt from her nose.

Debbie stood up and hugged her rescuer. "I saw a deer," she said, shaking the dirt from her hair. "I just wanted a picture."

Left to watch helplessly from the sidelines, Jon, David and Willy had never felt so helpless. As soon as the young women reached them, they grabbed them in bear hugs. Back on the trail, the campers were straining to see the action. Loud cheers went up as the group approached the path.

"What was it like?" Bill wanted to know. "Did you think you were going to die?" Rip asked. "You must have been scared!" Jo'Dee said. "You sure got dirty!" Vanessa offered. They all envied Debbie; it was too cool to fall into a sinkhole and be rescued! Jon's voice boomed over the noise. "Now you see why I told you all to stay on the path," he said. He put his huge arm around Debbie's shoulders, dwarfing her small stature with his great height. "Are you all right?" he asked. "Are you able to go on down to the cave?"

"I'm fine," she answered, smiling and rubbing a red place on her nose where a stick had nicked it. "Let's go!"

They resumed their single-file march toward the gorge. As they neared its edge, the canopy opened, bathing them in warm sunlight. Here the old leaves were dry, causing their feet to make loud, crunching noises as they walked. Because of this, they couldn't hear the sound of footsteps several yards behind them. So they didn't notice the person following them through the forest.

Chapter Ten

The Cave

Wagon Top Cave was an awesome and beautiful sight. The dark opening was forty feet high and almost thirty feet wide, wider at the top than the bottom. A crystal clear, cold stream slid between and bubbled over smooth golden rocks at the mouth of the cave. The climb down the mountain had been more of a slide down, the descent was so steep. Coming down such a radical incline is more difficult than climbing up. All the campers reached the bottom, and sat or lay along side the sparkling, dancing water, resting.

Rip lounged on a flat rock, tossing pebbles into the stream. He turned and tossed one into Vanessa's lap. "Stop that," she said, throwing it back. "You threw dirt down on my head all the way down the mountain. I'm tired of it."

"That's a lie!" Rip drawled. "I wasn't even above you. I was way down the mountain from you, wasn't I?" He turned to Tommy for confirmation.

"That's right," Tommy said smugly. Although he was finding girls more attractive as he grew older, he was still happy to prove a girl wrong.

"Well," Vanessa pouted, "*someone* was kicking dirt down on me."

"You were the last one last down the mountain, Vanessa," David said, stretching himself as he lay on his rock, hoping to end the argument. "No one could have kicked dirt down on you."

"After Debbie got *covered* with dirt and didn't complain, I think you can stand a little dirt on your head," Bill remarked. He was flat on his stomach, hand dangling in the stream. "I'm thirsty," he said. "Can we drink this water?"

"Absolutely not," David told him. "It looks good, but we don't know what kind of chemicals it may have in it."

Corbin was thirsty, too. This was one time she really hated to obey safety rules. The water looked so clear and fresh, it was all she could do not to taste it. Reluctantly, she pulled her water bottle out of her pack and took a swig. Seeing Bill staring at her, she said, "Did you bring some?"

"Na," he said, sheepishly. "I forgot it."

"Here," she said, handing her bottle across the rocks to him. "You can have some of mine."

Jo'Dee pulled a Coke out of her pack and started to open it.

"Jo'Dee," David shouted over to her. "Hold it. Don't drink that Coke."

"Why not," she asked, feeling a little angry, embarrassed at being told what to do. After all, she wasn't a child!

"Because if you do, you'll need to go to the bathroom about the time we're in the middle of the cave, and the caffeine will make you thirsty," David said with a laugh. "Did you bring some water?"

"I did," she answered, and pulled out a huge water bottle.

"I want to eat now!" Rip said. "I'm starving!"

"We don't need stomachs full of food," Jon said. "We're going through really narrow passages in the rock. We'll be bending and squeezing. You can have a snack, though." Standing, he called out in his loud voice, "Everyone be sure to drink some water before we go in, and you can eat something light like chips or a cookie or two."

All the campers eagerly scrambled through their packs to find some junk food to snack on.

"Be sure you close the packs up good," Jon called out. "We don't want to feed the bears our lunch!"

Rested, Corbin was anxious to get into the cave. "Who leads?" she asked Jon, standing and hooking her flashlight through her belt, she pulled on her blue helmet and patted her deep shorts pocket to be sure she had extra batteries.

"I think we'll let David lead," Jon said. "Next to me, he knows the cave best. I'll bring up the rear."

David was just as eager to get moving. He loved wild caves, especially this one. "Okay," he said. "Get your flashlights and lets go."

Corbin wanted Tommy behind her. "Come on," she said to him. "I want you close to me so we can talk."

"I've been in caves lots of times," he said, turning on and waving the huge flashlight his dad had loaned him. "This is going to be a breeze."

"Stick close, anyway," she told him. "I want company. And turn off that light. Don't waste your batteries."

David led off. Falling in line, they began their single-file trek once more, this time toward the black hole which was the mouth of the cave.

Just inside, huge pieces of broken grey rock were piled haphazardly, one on top of another, dropped there by some long-ago earthquake. The spelunkers climbed over them, bumping fingers and scratching knees against the hard, sharp surfaces. It was then that Tommy realized a wild cave was quite different from the ones he'd entered which had been prepared for public exploration. There were no gently sloping walkways carved out of the cave floor, and no hidden lights illuminating lovely, smooth stalagmites and stalactites. Instead, the broken rock pile grew higher and higher as they moved further into the darkness of the cave.

"I need my light," Tommy said. He had slipped down, and felt something gooey on his hand.

"Okay," Corbin answered. "It's time to turn it on." She pulled her flashlight out of her belt.

Rubbing his fingers on his shorts, he looked around at what appeared to be dark drops of something all over the rock. "What is this stuff?," he asked.

"It's bat poop," Rip laughed, shining his flashlight on the roof of the cave. "Look up." Hundreds of bats were hanging upside down, little toes clinging to tiny crevices.

"Yuck! Is the whole cave like this?" Tommy asked, struggling up and over a cold, grey slab, trying to avoid touching the darker matter. The rock was beginning to remind him of tombstones; he turned to look at the bright entrance, growing small behind them.

Bill caught the complaint in his voice. "No," he said cheerfully. "The whole cave isn't like this. It gets worse!"

"Don't pay any attention to him," Corbin laughed. We'll be on smooth rock in just a minute. See, we're going down, now." She flashed the light ahead of them, and Tommy saw that, indeed, they were beginning a descent. The broken rock fell away steeply just ahead, and he saw that they were too high up for his comfort. They must have climbed up more than forty feet and he hadn't realized it. He looked back. The light from the entrance had disappeared. All he saw behind him were the bobbing lights of his fellow spelunkers.

"How much further are we going?" he asked his aunt, trying not to reveal his discomfort about the height and his growing fear of being closed off inside the dark cave. "Is the rock going to fall anymore?"

In spite of his attempt to disguise it, Corbin knew he was worried. "It's okay," she told him. "I've been in this cave before, and so have David and Jon. That rock fell a long time ago. It hasn't fallen for hundreds of years. We're going to see some good formations pretty soon. There're some huge caverns, too."

"Great," Tommy said, only slightly hiding the sarcasm. "I can hardly wait." Unconsciously not wanting to move further from the cave entrance, he had begun to slow down, causing Bill to bump into his back.

"Go on," Bill said, a little irritated. "You almost made me drop my flashlight."

Looking about the caverns and not in front of him, Rip ran into Bill and dropped his light. It rolled and bounced down through a hole in the rocks, lost forever. "See what you made me do?" he screamed at Bill, shoving him into Tommy, who fell against Corbin.

"Whoa!" she said, catching Tommy's arm in her hand. She knew her nephew well, and whenever he was afraid he was prone to take a swing at someone. "No fighting!"

"Now what am I goin' to do?" Rip asked, almost crying over his lost light.

"Don't worry," Corbin told him. "Jon probably has an extra one. He usually does. Come on," she said to Tommy, "Give me a hand down these rocks."

Tommy swallowed his anger and took her hand. They used each other for balance to finish the descent. Once on the cave floor, his fear dissolved like a mouthful of cotton candy. The stream ran along the floor's center, disappearing under the rock pile. Tommy shone his light into it, enjoying the soothing play of the running water. He turned to meet Rip and Bill as they touched down on the cave floor. "I'm sorry, guys," he said. "It's my fault you lost your light." He reached out his hand, offering Rip his flashlight. "You can take mine."

"Oh, that's okay," Rip said. "I know this cave pretty well. I don't need it."

By now, Jon and his group were also gathering beside the stream. "Here," he said, smiling and pulling a long black object out of his pocket. "I always bring an extra one. It won't do for anyone to be in the cave without a light, experienced or not."

"Thanks," Rip said, smiling. He felt honored to carry Jon's light; he liked and respected the big man.

"Where are the others?" Jon asked.

"We slowed down some and David went ahead with them," Corbin said. "We can make up for lost time now that the going will be smooth awhile."

"Then let's do it!" Jon said, and they began to move quickly, walking at times on the side and at times through the stream, down into the bowels of the cave.

Corbin ducked under overhanging rock and rounded a curve, flashing her light ahead. She saw the tail end of the spelunkers who had outdistanced them, crossing the dry waterfall. Usually unafraid of heights, in this one spot Corbin, herself, became uneasy. The dry waterfall was made of smooth rock, formed thousands of years ago by water falling from hundreds of feet above them and into an abyss. No one knew how deep the pool below had been; their most powerful lights wouldn't penetrate to the bottom! And the water had dried up long ago. The rock was glassy smooth, but there was a slight ridge which jutted out just enough for a toe hold, so a person could inch across the waterfall to the cave floor on the other side, clinging to the slick rock with arms spread wide, fingers clutching small bumps and crevices. Willy was the last one in David's group to start the crossing. Corbin approached the dry falls and shone her light for him, careful not to allow the flashlight to dip, so Tommy wouldn't see into the depths below.

Before stepping onto the glassy surface of the falls, Willy had shone his light down into the abyss and was sorry he had. He had watched the light strain into the darkness beneath his feet, grow dim and die before reaching the bottom. While he wasn't afraid of heights, Willy knew he was a klutz! He couldn't imagine crossing the smooth, shining rock without losing his footing and falling. But not wanting the kids to think he was a coward, he had faced the slick rock and stepped off onto what seemed mostly air, toes clinging to the rim, arms spread and hands clutching whatever holds he could find, as he had seen the other campers before him do. Half way over, his hands began to sweat. He moved his foot to the right and stepped on nothing! For the first time in many years, Willy screamed. He pulled his foot back and found the narrow ridge again with his toe. And there he froze! He couldn't move at all.

David and the kids who had crossed the falls had moved on ahead, but Willy's scream brought them rushing back. David quickly moved over to the edge of the precipice and reached out for Willy's hand. He wasn't close enough to touch it. "Willy," he said, "Take some deep breaths. Just take it easy." He wasn't too worried; spelunkers had frozen here before, and he'd always been able to talk them across.

"I can't," Willy said softly but firmly. "I can't move." His voice was tinged with amazement as well as fear.

"You can make it," David said. "Just keep close to the rock, lean in and slide your foot just a little to the right. There's a nice ridge there; I can see it. You're almost to me. Just a few more inches and you'll be across."

"I can't," Willy said even more firmly. "I can't do it."

The two parties of spelunkers on either side of the precipice were at a loss. Willy wasn't going to move, and it wouldn't be safe to try and go out for him. It was likely that he would pull his rescuer down with him, like a drowning swimmer. Tommy played his light around the area, trying to think of something that might be helpful. He noticed a crevice in the falls just above and to the left of Willy's head. Moving his light along the smooth rock, running it back to his side of the falls, to his amazement he saw an opening about waist high in the cave wall next to him. While everyone watched Willy, Tommy stepped over to the opening and shone his light inside. It was big enough to crawl through,

and looked as if it wandered behind the falls.

"Corbin," he said. "Look at this." He grabbed his aunt's arm to pull her toward the opening.

"Not now, Tommy," she said. "We've got to think of a way to get Willy off the falls."

"But I may know a way," he pleaded. This was one of those times with Corbin when he felt like a child. Although she wasn't aware of it and didn't mean to, sometimes she made him feel like a bothersome little boy.

"What are you talking about?" she asked, turning toward the beam of his flashlight.

"I'm talking about this!" he said, scrambling into the opening. It was far too small to stand in, but it was large enough to scoot fairly comfortably on one's hands and knees.

"Come out of there," Corbin demanded. "This is no time to play around in tunnels. We need to help Willy."

Tommy regained his young manhood. "I'm *trying* to help Willy!" he said. "There's a hole just over Willy's head. I think this tunnel may lead up to it. If it does, he can climb in and won't have to go across!"

Corbin stepped back to the falls and shone her light over Willy's head. Sure enough, there was an opening in the rock just above and to the left of it. She turned back to Tommy in the tunnel.

"Get out of there," she said. "I'll climb up and see if it leads over to Willy."

"No way!" Tommy said. "This is *my* tunnel. I found it. I'll crawl it!"

Looking back at Jon, she saw he was too big to crawl through the tunnel, and she knew she was probably too light to pull Willy up. Although she was taller than Tommy, he was heavier and stronger. "Oh, okay," she said. "But don't get lost; watch where you're going."

She was talking to the air. Tommy was already shimmying through the hole in the rock, light dancing wildly in the tunnel as he pulled himself along on his elbows, all fear of close places forgotten in the excitement. He had a good sense of direction, and although the tunnel branched off in several places, he kept angling up and to the right.

Corbin returned to the side of the falls. "David," she called across the abyss. "Tommy's found a tunnel over here that he thinks might lead to the opening above Willy's head. Do you know anything about it? Have you ever been back there?"

"Yeah," David hollered back. "I forgot about it. It just dead ends, so we never use it." He noticed they were calling back and forth across Willy as though he weren't there.

"Tommy's gone up in it. Keep talking so he can hear us."

"Willy," David said in a loud voice. "Tommy's gone up a tunnel that opens over your head. Look up, a little to your left, and you'll see it."

Willy did as he was told, straining his head up and around. Although his skin was cold as a dead bat, he was still sweating. His hands seemed to have turned into rock; he no longer felt his fingers. But he saw the opening, about three inches above his left eye.

"Do you see it?" David called.

"I see it," Willy managed to whisper. He couldn't lock his knees, and his legs were trembling.

"Reach your left hand up, and see how far inside the opening you can get it," David said.

With a mighty effort, as though he were lifting up the mountain, Willy pulled his arm away from the smooth stone and moved his dead hand in the direction of the hole he'd glimpsed above his head. He couldn't locate it; he felt nothing above his wrist. Just as he was about to give up, Tommy's face appeared in the opening.

"Here I am, Willy," he said. "Give me your hand." Bracing his knees against the sharp rock, Tommy leaned out over the smooth rock of the falls. One of the campers was shining a light into the empty blackness below; Tommy suddenly realized he was leaning out over nothing! His hair stood on end and a chill ran the length of his body. There was nothing below him. Nothing! What if he fell into the abyss? What if Willy pulled him in? He was getting dizzy; sweat rolled off his forehead and down his nose.

"Tommy," Corbin called out. "You're there. Just reach down and Willy can grab your hand."

Now Tommy was frozen. All he wanted to do was crawl back down the tunnel and creep out of the cave. He couldn't do it. He couldn't reach out for the deputy.

But he wanted to reach out. He wanted to save the man. "Oh, Lord," he prayed, "I can't do it. Can you help me? Will you help me?"

Suddenly, Tommy saw a bright shimmering light surrounding Willy and the slick rock of the falls. It was if the cave were filled with shining water. The abyss was gone! Immediately, he knew the light was Christ. Jesus would hold him, wouldn't let Willy pull him out of the tunnel. He had help, all the help he needed. Reaching down, he grabbed Willy's left wrist and held it tight. Tommy's touch brought Willy back to life. He released his right hand's grip on the smooth rock, and moved it toward the boy.

"I've got you!" Tommy said, pulling Willy's arms into the opening. Now he was glad for his extra weight; it would help him pull the bigger man into the tunnel. Still holding Willy's wrists, he slid further back and braced himself with his feet on the sides of the rock walls. He still saw the shimmering light dancing all around Willy. "I've got you good!" he shouted with joy. "Pull yourself up."

All the spelunkers below shouted encouragement as Willy shinned up the smooth falls and disappeared into the tunnel. Once inside, he lay against the cold rock, catching his breath and slowing his pounding heart. Finally, he was able to look at the boy who had saved him. "I don't know how to thank you, son," he panted.

"Don't bother," Tommy replied. "It wasn't just me, anyway. Jesus helped." He had never felt so good, so complete, so at one with himself and with God. He turned around in the narrow tunnel, and began the crawl down to the cave floor, looking back occasionally to be sure his friend was following him.

While Tommy and Willy crept down the tunnel, the others agreed to end the caving there. No one believed Willy would be willing to try crossing the falls again, and they couldn't leave him alone. By the time the two popped out of the opening, the rest of the spelunkers had recrossed the falls and everyone was assembled on the near side.

"I'm sorry," Willy began to apologize to the group. "That's never happened to me before. I guess I'm too old a dog to try new tricks."

"Don't worry about it," David said. "Folks a lot younger than you have frozen here before."

"He's right," Jon said. "It happens almost every trip."

"He sure is right," Corbin chimed in. "The falls scares *me*. It's really the only thing in the whole trip that does."

Tommy wanted to tell everyone about the light, about how Christ helped him, but a voice inside told him to keep silent about it for now. Instead, he said, "That was fun. Willy and I got to see part of the cave you guys didn't."

Jon was ready to change the subject, wanting to save Willy any further need to talk about it. "I know what we should do," he said. "There's lots of room here. Let's sit along side the cave wall and turn off the lights. Has everyone done this before? Been in total darkness?"

Only Tommy hadn't had the experience, but the rest of the crew was ready for a rest, and experiencing the darkness was fun. Corbin found a place to sit. "Come on," she said to Tommy. "Sit here by me."

"I'm going to sit by Willy," Tommy said. Everyone found a place to sit, staying close together, touching each other. Jon sat down in the place Corbin had saved for Tommy and said, "When I count to three, off they go. One, two, three!"

All the lights went out at once. At first, an afterglow seemed to sit inside their eyes. Then, darkness and quiet settled in. Vanessa broke the silence.

"I've been thinking about it," she said. "Someone was above me on the mountain. I thought it was one of you, but if it wasn't, then who was it?"

"It could have been an animal," Bill said.

"I don't think so," Vanessa insisted. "It didn't *feel* like an animal."

"We need to be quiet to get the full effect of the dark," David said, although he knew the kids wouldn't get quiet again.

"Maybe it's the killer stalking us," Rip laughed.

"That's not funny," Jo'Dee said. Her eyes searched the darkness for Willy, but she could see absolutely nothing. "The killer couldn't know where we are, could he?"

Sensing she was speaking to him, Willy answered, "No, there's no way he could know where we are. I expect the sheriff's already rounded him up, anyways. His picture's been all over the county by now." He unconsciously felt for his gun, and was comforted when his fingers came in contact with the rough holster over the cold steel.

"We need to get a move on," Jon said. "It's getting late, and we need to be back to camp before dark." He turned on his light, beaming it toward the roof of the cave to avoid shining it in anyone's eyes. The rest of the spelunkers followed suit, and rose stiffly from the cold, hard floor.

The trip to the cave's mouth was uneventful until they came to the huge rock pile, where Tommy's foot slipped into a crevice in the rocks. He muffled a yell, then watched a huge, bleeding gash appear on his shin as he brought his foot up out of the hole. Jagged rock had removed the skin on his shin. He shrieked with pain when he gingerly put his foot down; he'd sprained his ankle as well! Glowing with pride as well as pain as he examined his bleeding leg, he realized he'd seen Christ, saved a man's life, and now he'd have a scar for life to remember it by. Corbin and Jon grabbed him under the arms and hustled him limping out the mouth of the cave. The rest of the spelunkers crowded up to get a look at the injury. They stood in the stream in the sunlight, watching David rinse the wound with the cool water. It wasn't until Jon headed over to get the first aid kit that they noticed the packs were strewn about, contents spilled out over the rocks.

CHAPTER ELEVEN

Another Uninvited Guest

"**G**ood grief!" Bill shouted, running up to his pack, Tommy quickly forgotten. "Someone's eaten my lunch."

"Somebody's eaten my lunch!" Rip yelled, racing up behind him.

Continuing this parody of the three bears, Vanessa cried, "And someone's eaten part of my lunch!"

"What in the world happened here?" Jon asked no one in particular.

"It looks like someone went through all the packs," Willy responded.

"But who would have done it?" Corbin wondered. "And why?"

"It looks like they were hungry," Bill said, reasonable as usual.

"They dumped out all the packs, though, not only the ones they ate the lunches out of," Calvin observed, gratefully finding his own lunch intact.

Rip was hoping for even more excitement. "It was a bear!" he said. "Is it still around?" He scanned the woods nearby, trying to sight the intruder.

David picked through the trash left from the sandwiches and chips. "No," he said. "It was definitely human. These sandwiches were unwrapped, not clawed."

Vanessa looked smug. "I told you someone was following us down the mountain," she said.

"You may have been right," David said grudgingly.

Calvin was stuck on his original question. "But why would he empty all the packs?" he asked once more.

Willy was almost unconsciously moving back into his sheriff's deputy role. "They were looking for something besides food," he said.

Jon looked at Willy, trying to fathom his thoughts. "What do you think?" he said, giving up on his attempt at extrasensory perception.

"My guess is he was seeing if there was some kind of identification in the packs," Willy said thoughtfully. "He may have been trying to find out who we are, something about us."

Corbin picked through the spilled contents of her pack. She tried to hold back her thought, but couldn't. She looked at Willy and said, almost in a whisper, "It was the killer, wasn't it?"

Willy wished she hadn't said what he was thinking. "We don't know that at all," he said. "It could have been anyone. Curious hikers, crazy kids, we don't know who it was. In fact, since we got the drawing of the killer out on the street, my guess is the sheriff has him safe in the county jail."

That the lunch thief might be the killer hadn't crossed Jon's mind, but now that the thought had been expressed, he wanted to find some way to reassure everyone. "Willy, where's your phone?" he asked. "Did you leave it in the van?"

"Nope," Willy smiled. "I've got it right here in my inside jacket pocket. I take it everywhere I go." He produced the little phone and flipped it open. The instrument began to beep gently. "Dang it," he frowned, dialing. "I hope I've got enough battery left." He stood silent a moment, listening to the distant ring. His smile broke out again as he heard the sheriff's gruff "Hello" at the other end. "Sheriff," he said, "this is Willy. I'm with the campers and we're at the mouth of Wagon Top Cave. We left our packs outside while we went in, and found 'em all tore up when we came out. Everybody wants to know what's happenin' where you are. Did you catch our man yet?"

The sheriff's voice came weakly through the little phone, which was beeping insistently. "Nope," Willy barely heard him say. "We got a make on 'im, though. He's a student, all right. Not a very good one. We've been through his quarters and found an interestin' iron, but not much else. And we know he drives a Bronco."

"So he's just a kid?" Willy said, relieved in spite of himself.

"Yea," the Sheriff said. "We checked him out with admissions. Name's Bobby Jones. He's just a punk, a sophomore. Got a rich daddy, though." The sheriff paused. Both were men of few words, and neither knew quite what to say next.

Willy bit the bullet. "Do you think he could've come down our way?"

"I don't know why he would," the sheriff drawled. "We're staking out his frat house. I notified the police in Arkansas where his daddy lives, in case he goes there. This here's a small campus. Some buddy could've told him we're lookin' for him. Anyways, I'll give you a call as soon as we get him."

"My phone battery's about out," Willy said. "But give me a try." He punched the power button to reserve what little supply was left, and crisply snapped the phone shut. Looking up at the campers staring at him, he realized they wanted more of an answer from him than he had to offer. "They've identified the boy," he said, sounding more hopeful than he felt.

"Who is he?" everyone wanted to know, voices rising in loud disharmony.

Willy told them everything the sheriff had told him, holding nothing back. "So, they're waiting to catch him as soon as he shows up at his frat house," he ended.

"If he's not there, he could be here," Bill said, ever logical.

"It's possible, but it's not likely he'd follow us. He doesn't even know who we are," Willy said, sounding as grumpy as the sheriff.

Corbin remembered yesterday at the campus restaurant, seeing the big, blond young man gazing across the darkened room at the sheriff and Willy, whose faces were lighted by the lamp in their booth. "He saw Willy in The Hangout. And Willy is with us!"

"That wouldn't matter to him," Willy said, tiredly. "If he knows the sheriff's after him, he wouldn't be worried about me. He'd hightail it out-a-town."

Tommy was following Corbin's thought, and became excited. "He might have seen us when we all ran out. He might have hidden in one of the shops and watched out the window. Maybe he knows Corbin and I saw him throw the man over the falls. Maybe he knows we know he's the killer." Everything that happened in the cave had made Tommy fearless. He felt indestructible, so the idea they might be stalked by a murderer was more thrilling than scary.

"Well, we're not going to find out like this," Jon said. He could see Tommy wasn't afraid, but Vanessa's face was white! "There's certainly not anyone around here now. Whoever it was is long gone. Let's eat. We've got a long hike back to the vans and we need to get to camp before dark."

"What about my leg?" Tommy asked, noticing the blood beginning to ooze again.

"I'm coming to bandage it right now," Jon said, picking up the first aid kit.

"What about my lunch?" Rip wailed.

"And mine," Bill echoed.

David asked everyone to divide up some of their food for their needy fellow campers. Vanessa was beyond any interest in food, wanting only to get out of the gorge, but she could see she was powerless over the others' hunger and decided at least to take the soda Jo'Dee offered her.

Although Tommy flinched a little when Jon wrapped his wound and bound his badly sprained ankle with a bandage, he was happy. He didn't feel the need to groan or make pained-looking faces. Before, when he was injured or sick he always performed theatrics to make it seem worse than it was. Corbin brought his lunch over to him, and he ate it ravenously.

The kids slowly began picking up trash and putting it in their packs. They hadn't realized how tired they were until they ate. Now they wondered if they could make it back up the mountain and hike the long trek to the vehicles.

"Can you call the hospital helicopter to come get us?" Bill asked. "I don't think Tommy can make it."

Willy laughed. "I don't think they'll come out for a sprained ankle."

Tommy looked at Bill, smiling at his pretended concern. "Don't worry, I can make it."

"Look around for a stick he can use," David said.

The kids found several, but Rip's was the best. He broke off two protruding branches to make a V at the top, like a crutch, and it fit Tommy's height almost perfectly. "Here you go," he said. "Try this on for size."

Tommy was delighted to have a crutch. He put the stick under his arm and tried to hobble around, but his ankle still hurt too much to walk on. Corbin came up and took his arm. "Can you walk now?" she asked?

He used her arm as a brace as well as his crutch, and was able to make some progress. "It's okay," he said. "I can make it."

"Are you sure?" Jon asked, looking doubtfully at Corbin.

"We can make it," she said. "You know it's easier going up than down."

"Then let's move out," Jon ordered.

Vanessa pushed into the middle of the forming line of campers. "I'm not going to be last again," she said definitely.

"Tommy and I'll be the tail on the dog," Corbin said.

"No, I'll come up under you," Jon said, "and give you a lift now and then. And I'll take your packs." Neither Corbin nor Tommy wanted to turn down that offer.

Everyone started the climb much less eagerly than they had descended.

CHAPTER TWELVE

A Shot in the Woods

Climbing up the gorge, Tommy couldn't hold back some shrieks as his ankle twisted inside the bandage. Corbin pulled him from above, and Jon occasionally had to boost him up from beneath. But they finally made it! When Corbin, Tommy and Jon's heads came up over the top, everyone else was lounging in the clearing. Exhausted, the three climbers dropped down spread eagle in the warm mulch, breathing hard, bathed in bright sunlight.

"Well, were you stalked by a crazed killer?" Rip asked jokingly, glancing at Vanessa.

"No sign of one," Jon said, with somewhat less humor.

"I feel all sticky and nasty," Vanessa said, changing

the subject. "Let's go on to the van. I need a shower."

"Give it a rest, Vanessa," Rip said. "We don't need to be in any hurry."

"It's all right," Corbin said. She, herself, was feeling ready for the showers, and she knew it would take Tommy and her longer to make the hike to the van. The swelling in his ankle was making the bandage look like a balloon. "You guys go on. We'll be right behind you. Jon, stay with the others. We're fine now. We'll holler if we need anything."

"If you say so," Jon said. He knew Corbin would be okay coming through the forest, and to try to stay back with them might seem like he didn't have confidence in her.

The hikers headed down the trail, David first, Jon behind Vanessa in the middle, and Jo'Dee and Debbie bringing up the end, just in front of Corbin and Tommy. The sun was starting to set, and as the group moved into the old growth, the tall trees' canopy blocked out more and more light. The air grew cool and damp, feeling good to the hot, tired hikers. As dusk fell quickly under the trees, insects began to tune up their instruments for the evening's concert.

Tommy was tired as well as injured. Although Corbin was helping hold up his weight, the stick under his arm was beginning to hurt more than help. He was moving more and more slowly. Finally he stopped altogether, panting and leaning on Corbin's arm. It was then that they heard the gunshot!

Just as the shot rang out behind them, Tommy felt a

sting and grabbed his ear. It was bleeding, and a tiny piece of it was gone! Without a word, Corbin grabbed him and threw him off the path. Keeping low, she put her hands under his arm and dragged him into the forest. She pulled him as deeply into the woods as she dared, mindful of the danger of sink holes. It wasn't difficult to find a huge oak to hide behind, and hope their assailant wouldn't look for them there. Tommy had the good sense to keep quiet; he was learning fast! They sat silently behind the ancient tree, trying not to breathe, wanting desperately to look toward the trail, but doing nothing to attract attention to their position. They heard the squish of heavy footsteps in the wet mulch. He was looking for them!

Corbin had never enjoyed playing hide-and-seek as a kid. She never won, and she was usually the first found. Now she prayed her luck had changed. She felt totally helpless, alone in the woods, unarmed, with a crippled nephew and a cold-blooded killer. She covered Tommy with her body, crunching him up against the tree.

Tommy knew better than to struggle. He could barely breathe, and thought he should just as well be the one protecting Corbin, but he sensed his aunt had almost reached the limit of her coolness, so he did nothing. He heard the footsteps moving about between them and the path, now away, now in their direction. Feeling Corbin's body stiffen with fear, he knew his aunt was terrified.

The footsteps came nearer to their tree. Corbin tried

desperately to think of a plan, anything to save them, but she couldn't. She couldn't call out for Jon, the man would kill them and be gone before anyone could reach them. She couldn't move fast enough, dragging Tommy with her, to run. Her brain felt like ice, frozen.

"Please, Lord, help us!" she cried silently.

Suddenly other sounds came from in front of and to the right of them; feet were running and voices whispering. Then they heard the heavy footsteps pick up speed and move away from their tree toward the new sounds. Corbin and Tommy listened intently, almost dying of curiosity, desperate to see what was happening. The sounds of running and whispering and the sounds of the heavy footsteps grew fainter. Obviously, the man was following someone else.

Debbie and Jo'Dee had been hiking just in front of Corbin and Tommy before the gunshot; tiredness and conversation had kept them from getting too far ahead. Unconcerned, the girls had watched the others disappear up the trail.

When they heard the shot ring out, they ducked automatically, and had the presence of mind to know someone was shooting at their friends. It had to be the killer!

Hugging the ground, Debbie whispered, "What do we do?"

"Call the others?" Jo'Dee suggested, keeping as low and invisible as possible.

"No time," Debbie thought out loud. The girls put

their heads up enough to see Corbin drag Tommy off into the woods, then watched as a large blond man in a flannel shirt and jeans, gun in hand, ran up to the spot where they left the trail and darted off into the woods after them. Since the danger was headed off in another direction, their racing brains kicked into gear. Jo'Dee looked at Debbie and whispered, "He'll catch them! They can't run, and Corbin can't drag Tommy far. We've got to do something." Jo'Dee looked heavenward, hoping for inspiration.

"I know what to do," Debbie whispered back. "You know the bird that distracts predators from her nest? What's its name?"

"I don't remember its name, but I know about the bird. It pretends to be hurt, and gets the bad animal to follow it."

Jo'Dee looked deeply into her friend's eyes. "Want to pretend to be a bird? Think he'll notice I'm black?"

"Let's do it," Debbie said. "Tommy's got a dark tan and his hair's black. He won't notice in this light. And I know exactly where to take him. Right toward the sink hole I fell in this morning."

The girls left the trail, scurrying through the forest in the dimming light, making noise but staying too low to be clearly seen, hoping to attract the killer and make him think they were Tommy and Corbin. They moved together, slightly north of the direction in which Tommy and Corbin had gone.

Whispering and running low to the ground, they paused occasionally to look behind them, peering through the dark trees, not knowing if their plan was working. Finally they saw him. They had his attention! He was coming in their direction. They ducked and Jo'Dee limped, trying to appear injured, moving in and out among the trees, heading for ground zero! The man was followed them through the woods.

Corbin and Tommy became brave enough to peek around their tree, and watched as the man moved through the growing darkness until he was completely swallowed by the forest.

"Wow," Tommy said, looking at Corbin in amazement. "I can't believe they did that. Who do you think it was?"

"I don't know, but we owe them our lives," Corbin answered. Never before had she felt such fear or such relief. In the cool twilight, her face ran with sweat. As her brain cells thawed, she realized what had happened. Someone in their group had decoyed the killer away from them. Others had risked their own lives to save them. "Let's go back toward the trail, Tommy. We can't help them alone. I'm going to hide you, then run ahead for Willy and Jon."

Tommy leaned on his aunt and hobbled along on his crutch as fast as his bad ankle would allow. He hated not to be present for the action, but he knew he'd be a hindrance if he tried to keep up or follow. "Okay," he said. "But don't forget where you put me."

Corbin had to laugh. "How could I forget you?" she said, seeing a huge rotting log with a crevice big enough to stuff her nephew in. "There," she said. "Crawl in there. And don't move, no matter what, no matter how long it takes, until I come after you." She pounded on the log with her boot, to run out any animals which might be hiding inside. Sure enough, something small, furry and fast ran out the hollow end.

Tommy ignored the pain in his ankle as he crunched himself into the log.

He hoped there wasn't a snake inside which hadn't been impressed by Corbin's thumping. Like his hero, Indiana Jones, he hated snakes!

Corbin threw leaves over the log where Tommy lay and ran for the trail, no longer cautious of sink holes. The path was nearer than she remembered, so she picked up speed, better able to see with light coming through the narrow opening in the giant trees.

Debbie was growing less sure about her bearings. It was really getting dark, and they had zigzagged a lot. She prayed she was headed in the right direction. A shot rang out. He was shooting at them!

"He's shooting at us," Debbie whispered.

"No kidding," Jo'Dee said as they slunk about under the trees. "If he hits us it'll be an accident. He can't see to shoot in this light, 'specially with us moving targets."

"I'll trust God that he's not lucky!" Debbie panted, breathless from running. "I'm not sure where we are."

"Wonderful," Jo'Dee responded. "We're lost in the deep, dark woods with a man shooting at us."

A monstrous scream rang out behind them. The girls

stopped in their tracks, turned and peered into the woods. There was no one to be seen. The man had disappeared. More screams seemed to come from underground. The screams turned into cries for help. *"Yea! Yes!"* the girls cried, jumping to their feet and high-fiving it. "He's in the sinkhole!"

Jon and the campers had heard the first gunshot, but assumed it was a tree branch cracking. The second shot was nearer and clearly identifiable, but in the forest it was difficult to tell the direction. The hikers stopped and looked around, giving Corbin time to catch up. She almost ran over Bill. Jon, David and the kids huddled around her, asking where Tommy was, wanting to know what happened.

"The killer," she said, hardly able to catch enough breath to voice the words. "Someone decoyed him away from me and Tommy. Now he's after them. I hid Tommy in a log."

Jon was big, and because of his size people sometimes thought he was less than intelligent. They were wrong. He was a genius. He knew immediately what had happened. "What direction?" he asked.

"That way," Corbin pointed east into the woods.

"This is where we went off the trail to the sinkhole," David said.

"Who's missing?" Jon asked, searching the faces turned up to him.

"Debbie and Jo'Dee," Rip said. "They were behind me."

"The sinkhole," Jon said. "They're trying to take him to the sinkhole."

"Of course," Corbin said, catching her breath. "Let's go!"

"David, take everyone on to the van," Jon said, fishing in his pocket, then tossing the younger man the keys. "Come on, Willy. Now that gun of yours may come in handy. Stay close behind me and don't fall into anything. Corbin, lead the way."

David hated to go to the van, but duty called and he was an Eagle Scout. He shooed the campers on up the dark trail. The kids were torn between excitement, fear and fatigue, and didn't resist as heartily as they would have earlier in the day.

Corbin was praying she was headed in the right direction, since it was too dark and too much had happened for her to remember exactly where the sinkhole was. Then they heard the screams, high pitched, but definitely male. No doubt now which way to go. He'd fallen in for sure. They moved fast in the direction of the cries for help.

Debbie and Jo'Dee had made their way carefully to the side of the hole. Debbie remembered the precious tree that held Corbin while she was being rescued, and seeing it, knew they would be on solid ground there. "Come on," she said. "The ground here is good."

The two girls moved up to the sinkhole. They could see nothing in the blackness, but they heard the man shouting and thrashing around inside. "Be still," Debbie called down. "Moving makes you fall in deeper."

The hole was quiet for a minute. "Is someone up there?" a doubtful voice came up.

"Yes," Debbie said. *"Don't move!* You're making things worse!"

"Who's up there?" the voice asked, wary now. What kind of help could a killer expect from his intended victims?

"Never mind who," Jo'Dee said. "We're going to get some help."

"No! Don't leave me here alone, please," the big man cried. He shifted his weight, trying to see his possible saviors, and slid several feet into the rock chimney, right up to his chest, dirt covering his head. At first he thought he'd been buried alive; it was an old nightmare of his. He yelled and sobbed, voice muffled by the dirt in his mouth, begging whoever was there to help him.

"Get the dirt out of your face," Debbie said, remembering her own plunge into the chimney. "You're okay. You won't fall any further now."

He didn't trust the small voice he heard coming from above him. Convinced he was buried and suffocating, he thrashed and squirmed, hopelessly locked in the crevice of rock.

"He won't listen to me," Debbie said, shrugging.

"Well," Jo'Dee said, "I'm listening, and I hear the others coming. They must have heard all the noise. We're over here," she shouted. "He's down in the hole."

At her words, Jon stopped and pulled out his giant flashlight. He wanted to be sure the gunman was incapacitated before they turned on any lights. Corbin and Willy followed suit. Debbie and Jo'Dee remembered they had flashlights themselves. They had been standing there hollering down the hole in the dark. Now the area was bathed in lights. Corbin rushed up to the girls and grabbed each in turn, hugging them tightly. "You saved us," she screamed. Grabbing hands, they jumped up and down like excited children.

It was minutes before they noticed the sobs issuing from the dark hole. "Oh, goodness," Debbie said. "I guess we'll have to get him out.

Jon took over the rescue and quickly located the rock Corbin had used. Since the man thought he was dying, Jon had to coax him to catch the rock and hold on to it. Willy helped Jon drag him up. As soon as he was halfway over the top, Willy reached down and snapped on the handcuffs. Then Jon and Willy dragged him the rest of the way out. The man lay gasping by the sinkhole while Willy tied his legs together, leaving just enough slack to allow the prisoner to hobble up the trail. Corbin stared into his face, wondering what made a man willing to kill, wondering if she could see something in his eyes that would help her understand. His blond hair was dark with earth; his blue eyes squinted in the flashlight's glare. His face was drawn from stress, and he looked just like hundreds of other college students. *"Tommy!"* Corbin suddenly thought. "We've got to get Tommy!" she said. "We've left him there way too long!"

"Can you get your prisoner to the van alone," Jon asked the deputy?

"Nothing easier," Willy smiled.

"Show me where you left Tommy," Jon said, and he and Corbin ran for the trail.

"Where? Where?" Corbin thought. "Please, God, let me remember where!" Everything looked strange as she shined the flashlight into the woods along the path, artificial light bathing branches and scattering shadows. *"Tommy, Tommy!"* she called as she ran. *"Come on out, it's safe!"* Jon's booming voice joined hers. *"Tommy, Tommy!"*

Rounding a curve, she saw what looked like a scarecrow in the middle of the trail. Tommy was covered head to toe in mulch. Jon ran up and grabbed him, picking him up and swinging him into the air, sprained ankle and all, sending the crutch flying.

"We got him, we got the killer!" Corbin shouted. "He fell in the sinkhole. It was Debbie and Jo'Dee who rescued us."

"Are they okay?" Tommy asked as Jon stood him gingerly on the ground.

"They're fine," Jon said. "Everyone's fine. Everything's fine!"

By the time Tommy, Corbin and Jon made it to the road, the sheriff was there. After talking to Willy, he'd been concerned about the weak phone battery. Not wanting to leave them without any means of communication, he'd come out to meet them. Everyone was delighted to see him; no one really wanted to have to ride with Bobby Jones. It would be hard to make small talk with someone who had just tried to kill your friends. Now, he was safely locked in the back of the sheriff's car.

Jo'Dee and Debbie ran for Tommy as soon as they saw him limp into the clearing. *"We got him!,"* they screamed. *"He fell in the sinkhole!"* "I know," Tommy hollered back at them. "You guys were *awesome!"* Unashamed, Tommy hugged them both and thanked them all the way to the vans. Now that everyone was together, there were so many separate stories to tell that no one could hear what anyone else was saying.

Jon heard Willy say something that caused him to call for order. "Settle down, guys," he said. "The sheriff and Willy need to take their prisoner in soon, and I want to know what's been going on. Willy, in all the commotion, did I hear you say the man confessed?"

Willy nodded, blushing with pride and embarrassment that he'd gotten his prisoner to talk. "Yeah, he confessed when we were coming back through the woods. It's not a pretty story," he said. "It was about drugs, just like we thought. He owed his dealer lots of money, and was scared to ask his dad for more. His dad was gettin' suspicious since he was askin' for so much money and his grades were awful." Willy stopped and scratched his chin, now nervous at having so many people's undivided attention.

"Go on, Willy," Jon said. "What happened."

"Well, the dealer came up and walked right into Bobby's dorm room; the door was unlocked. Lucky his roommate was out. The kid says the man had a gun and was fixin' to use it. Bobby'd been ironing some jeans—if you can believe anybody'd be ironing jeans—so he just come up and busted the man in the face with the iron. The kid said he didn't mean to kill him, but the man fell back, hit his head on the sink and died. The kid was so scared he decided to dump the body over Rainbow Falls. That's when Corbin and Tommy saw him."

"Then it was self-defense," Rip said.

"Shooting at Tommy and me wasn't self-defense!" Corbin said indignantly.

Willy looked apologetic. "He says he didn't mean to hit y'all, just scare you into not talkin' about him anymore. He says he's an awful shot."

Tommy touched his ear, feeling for the missing part. "He shot off my ear!" he said. "He sure didn't mean to improve my well-being."

"Well, he's committed plenty of crimes, and the lawyers and jury will sort it all out," the sheriff said. "In the meantime, he's gonna sit a long, long time in my jail. No judge in my jurisdiction is gonna give him bail. I can guarantee you that!"

"Come on, kids," Jon said reluctantly. "We've got to get in the vans. It's late, and we've still got to get to the campsite and fix supper."

"I'll need y'all to give statements," the sheriff said.

"We'll be happy to give statements tomorrow afternoon," Jon said, smiling at the kids. "In the morning, we're going rappelling off Jenkins's Steep."

CHAPTER THIRTEEN

Freedom

Jenkins's Steep is down a narrow blacktop road which is part of the campus. You drive down the house-lined street and are surprised when you see the edge of the mountain fall away and reveal the valley almost two thousand feet below. Even the kids who tried to appear the coolest were awestruck when they saw the view as the vans pulled into to the parking spaces where the road ends. They spilled out and ran straight for the cliffs, but Jon called them up short, making them help unload. Actually, it was all he could do to make himself wait. This was Jon's favorite part of the trip, and he thought there was no more beautiful sight anywhere.

The cliffs were forty to sixty feet high, made of the same golden sandstone as the buildings at the university. Strange, forty to sixty feet didn't sound so high until you got to the edge and looked over. Actually, at the bottom of the cliffs, there was only a ridge, just wide enough for climbers and rappellers to stand on. Below the ridge, the mountain fell away for over a thousand more feet before it transformed itself into a foothill. Beneath the cliffs, trees stretched themselves toward the sky, animals scurried, and mountain streams raced down the exposed rocks, singing as they went. The kids and counselors dragged the gear over to the clearing at the rock's edge, and began laying it out.

"Who's going over first?" Jon asked.

As usual, almost everyone spoke at once, everyone except Tommy that is. He was standing apart from the group, leaning on the crutch he'd carefully held onto throughout all last night's action. He was looking out over the precipice.

"What's up, Tommy?" Jon asked. "Don't you want to rappel?"

"Sure I want to," he said, "but I don't think I can with this ankle."

Corbin searched his face for signs of the old fear but didn't see any. He was standing closer to the edge than he ever would have before, and looked comfortable. "I know what you can do," she said. "We can let one or two kids go off here, then we can move a little further on where there's a free fall area. You can go down there. You won't hardly have to use your foot at all."

"Yeah," Rip said. "The free fall's fun. Last time we were here, one of the counselors turned upside down there and hung I don't know how long before she got herself right way up."

David laughed, "Don't let Rip scare you," he said. "We use two harnesses now, a saddle and a shoulder harness, so no one turns upside down anymore."

Tommy was relieved to hear this. "Okay," he said. "I'll watch a few minutes, then I'll go down." He sat down near the cliff's edge, to have a good view of the action.

Corbin, Jo'Dee and Debbie came and sat beside him. They all watched intently as Rip strapped himself into the harnesses and secured himself to the belay rope with a figure eight. Jon called out "Belay on," although he could clearly see it was. The formality was important to alert the rappeller to check the line and be sure he was ready.

"Belay on," Rip answered, and began stepping backwards toward the precipice. He looked down as his feet, gingerly edging his way to the cliff's edge. There, he made a last tug at the ropes and quietly began his descent. They watched in silence; although each one knew it was perfectly safe; seeing someone step off into nothingness is always fascinating. As he descended, Rip's body disappeared under the mountain. It would be several more minutes before he reached the ledge below.

Tommy looked around at the others. Pioneer Camp had changed them all. He thought about how Corbin, Jo'Dee and Debbie had been willing to sacrifice themselves for him, how Corbin, Jon and Bill had run off the

bear, and even his own desire to save Willy on the glass dry falls. On the Tennessee mountain they'd met evil; they'd seen life almost at it's worst. But they'd also discovered grace and goodness—the grace of God and the goodness inside themselves. They'd come to the mountain almost as children; they were leaving as much more. He realized all his theatrics and bragging in the past had been to hide his fear. He'd been just smart enough to know that alone he was powerless over much of the evil and danger in the world. What he hadn't known, what he hadn't understood, was that what he could count on was the power of God. One day soon, he decided, he'd tell Corbin and the others about seeing Christ in the light at the dry falls.

"Belay off," Rip called from below. Jon began pulling the rope up for the next rappeller. He looked at Tommy. "Ready?" he said. "Free fall is just a few feet away."

"Ready," Tommy said. He winced as he used his crutch to pull himself to his feet, then hobbled toward Jon.

"Here you go," Jon said. "Slip this harness over your head and put your arms through. That's right. Now your feet, just step into the lap harness."

"Which rope do I use for what?" Tommy asked.

"This heavy yellow one is the belay line," Jon said. "It's the one we tie your harnesses to with the figure eight. The blue one is your guide rope. You use the blue one to help keep yourself where you want to be once you go over the top. Remember, the harness and rope hold you as safe as if you were in a baby's cradle. Once you get a few inches over the side, the cliff falls back, and you'll feel like you're hanging a couple of thousand feet in the air, although the ridge is only sixty feet below you. Watch as you get near the ridge and use your blue rope to pull yourself onto it. Let me know when you get to the bottom."

"Is this right for the figure eight?" Tommy asked, pulling the rope through the metal clasp.

"Perfect," Jon said. "Belay on?"

"Belay on," Tommy responded, and began limping backwards toward the side of the cliff. Suddenly, his toe was on the ground but his heel was in the air. He was at the edge! The next step would be down, on the jagged face of the rock. He looked at Jon's face. The big man was concentrating on Tommy's movement and keeping just a little slack in the belay rope. Tommy's right foot swung off into nothingness as he leaned back into the harnesses which held him suspended in the air, then his good foot made contact with the side of the cliff. His left foot quickly followed suit. His climbing boots gave him support, the ankle was okay. Two more steps and he was in free fall. Swinging in the harness, almost two-thousand feet over the plateau below, he was free. His heart soared, he thanked God, and he knew he'd never be afraid of heights again.